PRAISE FOR
DAVID A. ROBERTSON

*David weaves an engrossing and unforgettable story with
the precision of a historian and the colour of a true Indigenous storyteller.*
—**ROSANNA DEERCHILD,** author and CBC Radio host
(praise for 7 *Generations*)

When We Were Alone *is rare. It is exquisite and stunning,
for the power conveyed by the words Robertson wrote, and
for the illustrations that Flett created.*
—**DEBBIE REESE,** American Indians in Children's Literature

*[David] manages to take on important and timely themes
while always keeping the reader engaged, engrossed and
entertained.*
—**SUSIN NIELSEN,** Governor General's Award-winning author
(praise for *Ghosts*)

*Once again, award-winning author David A. Robertson, a
member of Norway House Cree Nation, achieves a fantastic
balance between the development of the characters and the
pacing of the story to create a highly engaging read.*
—**SARA FLORENCE DAVIDSON,** BCTF Magazine (praise for *Ghosts*)

DAVID A. ROBERTSON

THE KODIAKS

HOME ICE ADVANTAGE

BOOK ONE OF THE BREAKOUT CHRONICLES

HighWater Press gratefully acknowledges the financial support of the Government of Canada and Canada Council for the Arts as well as the Province of Manitoba through the Department of Sport, Culture, Heritage and Tourismand the Manitoba Book Publishing Tax Credit for our publishing activities.

HighWater Press is an imprint of Portage & Main Press.
Printed and bound in Canada by Friesens
Design by Jennifer Lum
Cover art by Kagan McLeod

With thanks to the graphic arts student focus group from the MET Centre for Arts & Technology, Seven Oaks MET, and Maples MET (Winnipeg, MB) for their thoughtful feedback on the cover of this book.

CONTENT NOTE: This story includes scenes of racist behaviour and language that may be challenging to some readers.

Library and Archives Canada Cataloguing in Publication
Title: The Kodiaks : home ice advantage / David A. Robertson.
Names: Robertson, David, 1977- author.
Description: Series statement: The breakout chronicles ;
Identifiers: Canadiana (print) 20230534228 | Canadiana (ebook) 20230534236
ISBN 9781774921012 (softcover) | ISBN 9781774921029 (EPUB) | ISBN 9781774921036 (PDF)
Subjects: LCGFT: Sports fiction. | LCGFT: Novels.
Classification: LCC PS8585.O32115 K64 2024 | DDC jC813/.54—dc23

27 26 25 24   1 2 3 4 5

ENVIRONMENTAL BENEFITS STATEMENT
Portage & Main Press saved the following resources by printing the pages of this book on chlorine free paper made with 100% post-consumer waste.

TREES	WATER	ENERGY	SOLID WASTE	GREENHOUSE GASES
34 FULLY GROWN	2,700 GALLONS	14 MILLION BTUs	110 POUNDS	14,700 POUNDS

Environmental impact estimates were made using the Environmental Paper Network Paper Calculator 4.0. For more information visit www.papercalculator.org

FSC
www.fsc.org
MIX
Paper | Supporting responsible forestry
FSC® C016245

HIGHWATER PRESS
www.highwaterpress.com
Winnipeg, Manitoba
Treaty 1 Territory and homeland of the Métis Nation

THE KODIAKS

CHAPTER 1

ALEX ROBINSON had hoped this day would never come. For a while, it was distant enough that it hadn't actually seemed real. Like it wouldn't actually happen. But here it was. It was time to leave life as he knew it behind.

Alex loved his home in Norway House Cree Nation and would never have decided to move to the city, but he hadn't been given a choice. All he could do now was say a few goodbyes. And so, on the morning of the big move, Alex—or Robo to pretty much every hockey fan in the community—got out of bed before anybody else.

"We're leaving first thing," his dad had said last night before Alex went to bed.

"Can't wait to go or something?" Alex had asked.

"No, that's not it. It's just like ripping off a Band-Aid," Dad had said, pretending to rip a Band-Aid off his arm. "The quicker you do it, the less it hurts."

Alex threw on some clothes, then glided through the house towards the front door, avoiding the creaky spots. He knew every creaky spot. After all, he'd lived there his entire life.

Safely outside, Alex rolled his bike down the driveway and jumped on when he reached the street. From there, he rode through Rossville, the main area of the reserve, towards the multiplex. The multiplex housed the radio station, a restaurant, the drop-in centre, the gym—and the hockey rink. The rink was what Alex needed to say goodbye to. It had been his second home ever since his mom strapped double-bladed training skates onto his boots and led him onto the ice.

He didn't need those skates for very long.

"You were a natural," his mom often told him.

Getting from one place to another in Rossville was quick. Other areas of the rez were sprawled out, but Rossville was like any small town. The multiplex, the hotel, Chief and Council's office, the mall, the gas station, and the school were all within a ten-minute walk. Alex biked into the multiplex parking lot and stopped near the entrance he'd walked through a million times before.

He lowered the kickstand and took a few steps towards the building. He wished he could go inside, but the doors were locked. He wished he could walk out onto the ice one last time. His dad once told him how he'd gone to centre ice and touched the red circle when the Winnipeg Jets left the city for Phoenix. An avid hockey fan, he said it had given him closure.

Alex imagined doing the same thing. He pictured himself walking across the ice towards the red dot. He pretended he could hear the roaring crowd. This was all easy to do because he knew the rink like the back of his hand. Still, it wasn't the same.

He could see into the lobby from where he was standing. On game nights, it was packed. But nobody was there this morning. All Alex could see was his reflection. When he waved goodbye to the arena, he was waving goodbye to himself. It was like he was leaving part of himself behind.

A flood of memories hit him. Every single moment he'd ever experienced on the ice and in the dressing room with his teammates swirled around in his brain. He thought of the long trips they'd taken to play all over Manitoba. That's when they all became friends. When they were on the road, they spent every second together. He knew that hockey teams didn't travel much in the city. A road trip for them was thirty minutes, not, like, eight hours. Alex doubted teams went to other rinks on a bus. They probably went separately, in their parents' cars. And how many Indigenous kids were on those teams?

"Some people are going to think they know you, even if they've never met you before," his dad had told him one night as they were packing.

It had felt like a warning.

Alex kicked at some loose stones on the concrete and watched them skitter off. He looked through the front doors into the lobby one last time, trying to soak up all the good memories, so he could take them with him. Then he got back on his bike and pedalled away, wondering if he would ever play there again.

CHAPTER 2

ALEX RODE UP AND DOWN each street, waving at every car that passed. It made him feel good that people waved back. Alex knew why. The whole rez knew he was leaving. Alex was the best player on the hockey team. He had the most goals and the most points, played every penalty kill and every power play, and he was on the ice in the last minutes whenever the game was on the line. Last season, the North Stars won the championship and Alex was the MVP.

A passing car stopped. The driver rolled down his window.

"Give 'em heck down there in the city, Robo," the man said, raising his fist.

"I'll do my best," Alex said.

"Ekosi!" the man shouted, which meant "Way to go!" in Cree, then kept driving.

Alex biked on, pedalling more deliberately towards his last stop. He'd put it off as long as possible, but now it was time to say goodbye to his best friend.

Alex had been pretty much brothers with George all his life, since before he could skate. Their parents had been friends forever, so they were destined to be friends, too. It helped that they actually liked each other, and that George also played hockey. He was Alex's linemate. Whenever Alex was on the power play or penalty kill or making a play in the final seconds of a game, George was right there with him. On the ice he was known as Cap because his last name was Captain.

Alex turned sharply into George's driveway. His tires crunched against the gravel and kicked up a cloud of dust. He dodged toys left out by George's younger siblings, then skidded to a stop at the front door. Alex checked the time. It was still early. To spare George's parents a wake-up call, Alex walked around the side of the house with a handful of gravel and tossed the tiny stones at George's window. George stuck his head out into the chilly morning air.

"Tansi, boy," George said.

"Tansi to you, too," Alex said.

"Ho-lay," George said. "When you told me you were coming early, you weren't kidding."

"We're leaving first thing," Alex said. "When else was I going to come?"

"Hang on a sec," George said.

He disappeared, and Alex waited there, leaning on his bike. Moments later, George jogged around the corner of the house, holding a hockey stick. Alex recognized it as George's favourite stick. It was a Warrior QRE 50 - 40 Flex.

"Ever whippy," George had said when he started using it last year.

It was an amazing stick and it looked cool, too. It had a blue blade, a blue-and-black handle, and WARRIOR printed in orange down the middle.

"Cap," Alex said, "I don't have time to play road hockey." He looked at George's stick, which was in pristine condition. George took care of his Warrior like a newborn baby. He never took slapshots because he didn't want to break it. "You wouldn't use that on the road anyways."

"I don't want to play road hockey," George said. He held the stick out towards Alex, cradling it in his open palms. "This is for you."

Alex pushed it away. "No way! I can't take your stick, Cap. Forget it!"

George pushed the stick against Alex's outstretched hands, and it became like a reverse tug-of-war match.

"You *can* take my stick because I'm giving it to you," George said. "You're going to need it down there with all those city kids."

"But this is your favourite," Alex said. "You've literally told me that. You've told me that you never had a better stick."

George shrugged. "I never had a better friend."

Alex stopped resisting.

"I actually think there's something cultural about accepting gifts and stuff like that," George said.

"Pffft," Alex said. "Not even."

The boys laughed loud enough to wake up everybody in George's house.

"I'm gonna miss you," Alex said once they'd stopped laughing.

"I know," George said.

As Alex held the stick, he pictured all the times George had used it to pass the puck or score. Almost every time, he'd passed to Alex. Or Alex had passed to him. Who was going to pass to Alex now?

"I can't believe it's already almost tryouts," Alex said. "I bet there's going to be one thousand kids going for the same team. That's what my dad said anyways."

"Don't worry even if there are ten thousand kids, Robo," George said. "You got this."

Alex rolled the stick over his palms, back and forth, letting the sun glint off the smooth surface.

"What if I don't?" Alex asked.

George looked Alex dead in the eye, then poked his finger against Alex's chest.

"Dude, there'll only be one warrior out there," George said.

"Cap, lots of kids use Warriors," Alex said.

"You know what I mean," George said.

"You think I'll be the only Native kid trying out?" Alex asked, suddenly feeling anxious. He could hear his dad's voice: *Some people are going to think they know you, even if they've never met you before.* Had it really been a warning? What would everyone be thinking about him? How could a stick protect him against that?

"You never know," George said. "Either way, you've totally ruined my pep talk."

"All right, I'll be a warrior." Alex pushed aside his worry and tried to look confident. "Happy?"

"You're lucky," George said. "I was about to take it back."

"I think there's something cultural about taking *back* gifts, too," Alex said.

"That's not cultural, that's just rude," George said. "And I'd never take it back. It's yours."

"Ekosani," Alex said. "Thanks."

He promised George that he'd call him that night when he got to the city. That he'd call every night, no matter what.

$$X$$

When Alex got home, his parents were awake and sitting at the kitchen table, surrounded by moving boxes and eating bowls of cereal. They told him they'd gotten up after they heard him leave the house. He wasn't as quiet as he'd thought.

"Weren't you scared I was going to run away because I don't want to move?" Alex asked.

"Where would you go?" Dad asked, chuckling.

"I don't know," Alex shrugged. "To the trapline?"

"We'll still go there," Mom assured him as tears welled up in Alex's eyes. Moving was real now. It was getting more real with each passing second. "This place will always be our home."

"Promise?" Alex asked.

Dad walked over and put his hand on Alex's shoulder.

"Promise," he said. "I know you were off saying good-bye, but you know what? There's no word for 'goodbye' in Cree for a reason. We'll visit all the time."

"Do you think one day we can move back?" Alex asked.

"I hope so," Dad said. "It depends on if the school gets better funding, and if I feel like I can do more good here than at my new job in the city. Either way, I've got to give it a shot."

Alex wiped his eyes with the sleeve of his hoodie and nodded. With his tears at bay, he showed his parents the stick George had gifted him. They talked about hockey after that, forgetting, even with boxes all around them, they were moving at all. But soon it was time. They finished breakfast, packed up the rest of the trailer, and hit the road for Winnipeg. Alex looked out the rear window as the community got smaller and smaller, until it disappeared. Then he stopped looking back and started to look forward. It was late August and tryouts were only a few weeks away. If his dad was giving it a shot, he would too.

CHAPTER 3

T HE NEXT FEW WEEKS passed quickly. Time always went by fast when there wasn't a moment to breathe, and that's exactly how Alex felt.

First, they moved into their new house. It was a green house in an area of the city called the West End. Alex thought the name was funny because the neighbourhood was closer to the centre of Winnipeg. The house looked pretty big when he first walked inside, but it felt a lot smaller when it was filled with boxes and furniture—as small as Alex felt in the city. The rez was big, but there was so much open space. Winnipeg was way bigger, and the countless buildings and houses were crowded together like the moving boxes in Alex's new room.

There were a lot of kids on the street, and Alex joined them in a game of street hockey while his parents unpacked. At the end of the street there was a convenience store that had candy and soft drinks. It made the move a little easier to take.

Then it was the first day of school. Alex was starting grade 6. In Norway House, he'd gone to the Helen Betty Osborne Ininiw Education Resource Centre, the school where his dad had worked. Now he was going to a school called Sargent Park. It seemed like a maze compared to his old school.

"It probably just seems confusing because it's new," his mom said after his first day, when he came home looking, according to her, overwhelmed.

Alex figured out his way around the school, but he found it hard to get used to the kids in his class. They seemed nice but he was nervous to talk to them. Most of them laughed when he got in trouble for not looking at the teacher when the teacher was talking to him. Alex got sent out in the hall for five minutes for being disrespectful.

"Even though there are other Native kids at school, the teachers may not have had a kid from the rez before. They don't know about our cultural traits," Mom said. "You just have to tell your teacher that you didn't make eye contact because it's a sign of respect for authority."

"Son," Dad said, "I know it's hard being in a new place, and it feels harder when people don't understand you. But sometimes you can help them understand."

Alex didn't feel comfortable talking to his teacher about it. He thought his teacher would get annoyed with him. From then on, Alex tried to look at his teacher when he was speaking, and he didn't get sent out of the room again.

Next Alex had to get used to how different living in Winnipeg was from living on the rez. Alex had visited the city a few times before they moved, but never saw much of it. He and his parents drove around to figure out where everything was. They even took the bus one day. Alex thought that was fun because he'd never been on a bus before, not a city bus anyway. The North Stars had taken a team bus when they travelled to other communities like Opaskwayak Cree Nation or Thompson to play games. But when he was on that bus, people didn't look at him funny. On the city bus, the way people looked at him and his parents made him feel bad, like they didn't belong.

"Is this what you were telling me about?" he asked his dad. "About people thinking they know us?"

"Yes," Dad said.

"How do I make them not look at me like that?" he asked.

"I don't know." Dad sighed. "But I do know this: You don't have to change who you are for anybody."

Finally, it was time for tryouts. Alex couldn't wait to get on the ice and do something that felt normal. There was no hockey team in the West End because there weren't enough kids that played, so Alex had to play in a neighbourhood called St. James.

"Our arena is bigger than this one," Alex said as his dad parked the car at Allard, the arena where tryouts were being held.

"I guess some things aren't bigger in the city, hey?" Dad said.

Alex got out of the car, opened the trunk, and took out his hockey bag. He slung it over his shoulder.

"I guess not," he said.

He reached for the Warrior, sliding it out of the trunk as if he were taking a sword out of a sheath.

CHAPTER 4

WHEN ALEX AND HIS DAD walked in, the lobby was swarming with hockey parents and players. The line to register for A1 extended all the way from the rink doors to the arena's entrance. They went to the back of the procession and shuffled forward, inch by inch. The smell of popcorn wafted through the air, and popped kernels littered the ground like freshly fallen snow. By the time they reached the registration table, it was thirty minutes until Alex's ice time.

After registering, Alex followed his dad into the rink, where a different group was on the ice trying out. The crunch of steel against ice and the clap of sticks against pucks filled the arena. Parents were pressed up to the glass all along the boards watching, coffee cups in hand. There was a skate-sharpening booth beside two vending machines, one machine for drinks and one for snacks.

There was a donation bin full of used hockey equipment. It was all familiar to Alex. No matter how different one place was from another, hockey was the same everywhere.

Alex's dad headed for the stands and Alex made his way to the dressing room. When he opened the door, he found the room almost full. He spotted one empty space beside a red-headed kid who looked like he was having the time of his life, as though a smile had been tattooed on his face. Alex lugged his bag over, sat down, and began rummaging through his equipment to find his jock. He hadn't even put it on before the red-headed kid punched him lightly on the arm.

"Hey," the kid said.

"Hey," Alex said, pulling on his jock shorts, then grabbing a shin pad.

"What's your name, bud?" the kid asked.

Alex strapped on one shin pad and then the other. "Alex. Alex Robinson."

"You just said your name like you're a secret agent."

Alex paused before answering. "Maybe I *am* a secret agent," he said. "I could be here undercover on a top-secret mission. You never know."

"What sort of top-secret mission would happen at a hockey rink?" the kid asked, playing along. "Is one of the players an internationally wanted criminal?"

"That's classified," Alex said.

"Well," the kid said as they both pulled their pinnies on over their equipment, "I know what your code name should be."

"Oh yeah?" Alex said. "What's that?"

"Robby," the kid said matter-of-factly.

Alex repeated *Robby* in his head a bunch of times. Then he alternated between *Robby* and *Robo*, his hockey name back on the rez.

"That's not bad." Alex shoved his feet into his skates. He tied them so tight that by the end of the tryout he wouldn't be able to feel his toes. He noticed that the red-headed kid was doing up his skates super loose. "Why do you do it that way?"

The kid shrugged. "My dad told me it would make my ankles stronger, but now I do it because I'm used to it."

Alex put on his helmet and gloves. He picked up his stick and leaned against it as if he needed it for support. He checked the time. The tryout was starting in a few minutes. He could hear the Zamboni cleaning the ice.

"What's your name?" Alex asked.

"Aidan," the kid said. "Wuerfel. You can call me Wuerf."

"Wuerf?" Alex said. He liked the ring of it—it rhymed with Nerf. He didn't mention that, however. He was sure Aidan had heard it countless times before.

"That's what I've been called since I started playing hockey. I get called Wuerf more often than Aidan now."

Alex looked down at his skates for a moment and pretended he was in the dressing room at the Norway House multiplex. It had the same black rubber flooring.

"Back home I got called Robo," Alex said.

"Like, as in *RoboCop*? That's awesome!" Wuerf said.

He stuck out his glove for a fist bump, so Alex did, too.

"I guess," Alex said. "I actually never thought of that."

Alex felt like he was making a friend. Well, a hockey friend. He thought of George, back on the rez. That was his *best* hockey friend. Being friends with somebody else felt a bit like betraying George. Alex thought of a conversation he'd had with his parents on the way to the city.

"I don't want to play on a new team," he'd said out of nowhere. "I like the team I was on."

"I know it's hard to leave friends behind, especially a friend like George," his dad had said. "But you'll make new friends, and eventually they'll feel like family to you."

Was this new kid going to feel like family to Alex? Both of them had to make the team first. Alex thought he had a pretty good chance, but he had no idea if Aidan was decent. He could've been an ankle-bender for all Alex knew, especially with those loose skates. But what did that matter? If Aidan was bad, it didn't make him any less friend-worthy.

A man wearing skates, sweats, and a blue team jacket opened the door to the dressing room. Alex noticed a white logo on the jacket. He leaned forward and squinted, trying to see what it was, and finally concluded that it was the head of a bear.

"You boys ready?" the man asked.

Alex figured he was a coach. All the boys responded enthusiastically, except for Alex, who'd returned his gaze to his skates and the rubber floor underneath his blades.

"We're on," the man said.

He left the room just like that. Before the door closed, Alex saw the team name on the back of his jacket.

Kodiaks.

The dressing room cleared quickly as the kids filed out one by one, then lined up inside the boards from the gate to the goal light. Alex and Aidan were at the back of the line. They'd taken an extra minute to leave the dressing room because Aidan started quoting RoboCop lines, in a RoboCop voice. As they waited to get on the ice, Wuerf glanced back at Alex and said, "I still like Robby though, because I made it up."

Alex liked it too. He wasn't in Norway House; he was in Winnipeg. Keeping his hockey name would make him miss home more than he already did. If he was going to make the team, he didn't need a distraction like home-sickness. Like it or not, this was a new start, and having a new name made sense.

The coach with the Kodiaks jacket opened the gate and the kids burst onto the freshly cleaned surface. As if sparked to life by the sound of skates digging into ice, Alex's heart started to beat hard and fast.

"Ready to rock, Robby?" Wuerf asked as they moved closer and closer to the gate.

"Yeah," Alex said before stepping onto the ice. "I'm ready."

CHAPTER 5

A
S THEY SKATED slow warm-up laps around the ice, Aidan explained to Alex that every kid trying out got three skates to show what they could do. After that, the team was chosen. One of the coaches blew his whistle, signalling that the tryout was about to start. He told the players to line up in four lines, facing cones that had been placed on the ice in a zigzag pattern. Each player had to stickhandle around the cones, then skate at full speed back to where they'd started. Alex had done the same thing a thousand times in Norway House.

Some of the players made the drill look easy, but others bumped into cones or lost the puck and helplessly watched it slide away. Alex cringed when that happened, feeling bad for the player while imagining himself making a similar mistake. When the player in front of him bumped into a cone *and* lost the puck, everybody's worst nightmare, Alex looked away as if he'd witnessed a car accident. After each kid had gone through the drill, one of the coaches began tapping on a tablet, ranking their performance.

Soon it was Alex's turn. He gave his Warrior stick a squeeze as if encouraging it to perform well, then took off at the whistle. He navigated past each cone with tight turns, keeping the puck on his stick as if it was glued to the tape. When he passed the last cone, he turned back and raced towards the end boards at top speed, pushing the puck in front of him with each stride. He loved the feeling of wind rushing against his face and hearing his jersey flap like a flag as he streaked down the ice. Right before he hit the end boards, he did a hockey stop and sprayed snow, blocking the view of two parents. For a moment the glass looked like a window streaming with rain. As Alex took his place at the back of the line, he watched one of the coaches tap his tablet. What score had he been given?

"Who are you?" the kid in front of him asked.

"Alex," he said.

"That was sick," the kid said.

"Thanks," Alex said. "Uhhh, what's your name?"

"Johnny," the kid said, then added, "Ryan Johnston."

He'd said his name like a secret agent, too. It was a thing.

Alex's second turn through the cones went about as well as his first, although halfway through he almost lost the puck and worried that the coach noticed. He felt like any mistake could cost him a spot on the team. When he finished, he watched Wuerf. He wasn't as fast as Alex, but he controlled the puck and had a powerful stride, like a charging bull. Alex decided right then that Wuerf would probably make the team.

After more drills testing stickhandling and speed, they finally got to shoot. The coaches put the kids in two lines, one on either side of the goal, and placed a puck at centre. When the whistle blew, the kid at the front of each line skated as fast as they could to the puck, and the first one to get it kept going towards the other goal. The player who lost the race had to try and stop the player with the puck from scoring.

Some of the matchups were uneven and some were super close, like a photo-finish at a horse race. The battles for the puck were so intense that often neither player got to shoot. When Alex got close to the front, he looked at the other line and noticed that Wuerf was next in line, too. He smiled at Alex as they lined up. Alex and Aidan got into racing stances as if they were about to do a 100-metre dash. The whistle blew, shrill and sharp. Alex pushed off with his back foot and barrelled towards centre ice. To Alex's surprise, Wuerf was right with him.

Alex reached the puck just ahead of Wuerf. He could hear Aidan's skates churning up the ice behind him, hot on his heels. Alex turned on the jets and streaked towards the net. As he crossed the blue line, Wuerf hooked at Alex's arms with his stick. Alex did his best to fight him off while maintaining control of the puck. When he was a couple of feet away from the goalie, he flipped the puck into the air one-handed, his other hand occupied with Aidan's stick. The goalie snagged it out of the air before it crossed the goal line.

Alex looked up in disbelief.

Aidan patted him on the shoulder and said, "Good battle, Robby."

"You too," Alex said. "Almost got me."

"I *did* get you," Aidan said. "Mostly."

When it was time for the scrimmage, the coaches split the kids into two teams, yellow pinnies against green pinnies. Alex and Wuerf were both on the yellow team. Alex started the game on the bench and scanned the arena from left to right while he waited to jump over the boards. His dad, squished in the stands, looked nervous like all the other parents. Hockey parents were always nervous. Hockey parents were even nervous at practices. Hockey parents were weird.

After the first shift ended, it was Alex's turn.

He was left-handed but played on the right wing. For the faceoff, he lined up against the boards, and Wuerf took the centre position. The coach dropped the puck and Wuerf won the faceoff, sliding the puck to the defenceman. He fired a solid pass to Alex, who deked around a green player and cleared the blue line, then passed to Wuerf. Alex charged up the ice, and when they entered the offensive zone, Aidan hit him in stride. Alex cut towards the net. Out of the corner of his eye, he saw the left-winger wide open and fed him the puck. The kid had an open cage but somehow missed. The puck hit the glass behind the net and rimmed around the boards. As Alex turned to chase the puck, he saw a flash of green before everything went black.

It took Alex a couple of seconds to get his bearings. Not only had his back hit the ice but he was pretty sure his head did, too. He stared at the arena lights blazing down on him, white and intense. It was like he'd died and gone to heaven. There were the lights and nothing else until helmets blocked his view, and Alex knew he was alive. He blinked a few times and the lights got less bright.

"You okay, Robby?"

Wuerf offered a gloved hand to help Alex to his feet. Alex checked whether his head was still on his shoulders, then reached out to Wuerf. As they moved slowly towards the bench, a player in a green pinnie skated in front of them without stopping.

"Better watch where you're going, Chief," he said.

"What was that for?" Wuerf asked. "Are you serious?"

The kid smirked and headed for the bench.

"I guess that's the kid who hit me," Alex said to Wuerf.

"Yeah, that's Terrence." Wuerf's tone was confused and shocked all at once. "He's aggressive, but not usually like that."

"I feel like I ran into a brick wall," Alex said groggily.

"More like the wall ran into you," Aidan said.

Alex took a seat at the end of the bench and drank some water before pouring a bunch on his head. The coach skated over and gave him a pat on the shoulder.

"Alex, right?" he asked after checking his tablet. "How're you feeling?"

Alex shrugged. "Like I got hit by a truck."

"Well, listen," the coach said. "I'll deal with it. You better head to the dressing room and talk to your parents. I'll call tonight to see how you're holding up."

Alex nodded. "Okay, Coach."

The coach patted the board and nodded at Alex, then skated off. When Alex got up, he felt pretty solid on his feet, but he knew his dad wouldn't let him try out tomorrow. The coach probably wouldn't let him either. For a second he wondered if that would hurt his chances, but nobody would cut him just because he'd taken a dirty hit. Plus, the coach knew his name. That had to be a good sign.

CHAPTER 6

ALEX WAS QUIET during the car ride home. His head was sore but not that bad. He was more upset that he couldn't finish the tryout than worried about his head. He'd hardly played one shift! He knew accidents happened on the ice and kids collided all the time. But that hit must have been intentional. If it wasn't, Terrence wouldn't have said what he'd said.

Better watch where you're going, Chief.

Alex's mom had put together a "tryout meal" for when he got home. It was a feast more than a meal. His plate was filled with bannock, moose meat, mashed potatoes, and mixed vegetables, and there was pie for dessert. But Alex didn't feel like eating. That, more than anything, made his parents worried. After supper they searched online to see if lack of appetite was a concussion symptom. They asked him a million times if he was nauseous, but he didn't feel nauseous. What Terrence said bothered him so much that he didn't feel like eating anything. He had a spoonful of potatoes and a forkful of moose meat, then asked to be excused.

In his bedroom, that name kept repeating in Alex's mind. *Chief.* There was only one Chief, as far as he was concerned. The actual Chief of his community. Terrence had been making fun of the fact that Alex was Indigenous. Cree, to be specific. His dad had always told him to be specific about who he was, and more importantly, to be proud of it. And Alex *was* proud. But now somebody had hit him because of it. He felt all mixed up, and not from hitting his head. He'd left his hockey bag by the front door but brought his stick to his room. He lay in bed with it as if it was a stuffed animal he needed for comfort. *Warrior.* He wouldn't have minded being called Warrior.

Even though his parents had told him not to look at any screens to give his head a chance to rest, Alex picked up his tablet and called George.

"Robo!" George said. His face froze with his eyes closed and his mouth open, which made Alex chuckle. "What's going on?"

The video was choppy. The Wi-Fi and cellular connections back home were bad and when they chatted, half the time George looked normal and half the time he looked like he'd been paused. At least his voice was clear.

"Hey Cap," Alex said, then brought George's stick on-screen. "I haven't broken it yet."

"How was your tryout?" George asked.

"It started off awesome," Alex said. "All the drills and everything."

"And then?"

Alex's chest felt hot, thinking about what had happened.

"And then I got hurt."

"What?" George's face froze in a look of worry. "What happened?"

Alex rubbed his head where it was sore.

"Some big kid threw a deadly hit. Just totally blind-sided me." He clapped his hands together to demonstrate.

George's face unfroze but he still looked concerned. "It's no contact in the city, isn't it? It's no contact on the rez."

"It's *supposed* to be no contact," Alex said.

"So why'd he do that then?" George asked. "I totally would've taken him out for you."

"The guy who did it called me Chief."

George nodded. "One time in the city somebody said that to my dad. He got so annoyed."

"*I've* never been called something racist like that before," Alex said.

"You've never played hockey in the city before," George said. "Hopefully that's all they call you."

"I know a lot of people don't like Natives, but I didn't think a kid would say something like that."

"I guess *that* kid would say something like that."

"Like, out of all the things I've been worried about, I wasn't thinking about getting hit because I'm Native."

Alex and George fell silent. For a moment it looked as if they were both frozen, like they both had terrible connections.

"So, what now?" George asked.

"Now I bet I can't even try out tomorrow," Alex said. "The coach is supposed to call tonight."

"So does that mean you're gonna have to play A2 or something?" George asked.

"I hope not," Alex said. "I think I could skate circles around some of the kids who'll be playing A2."

"Let me know how it goes," said George, who hadn't frozen for a long time.

It felt like a good time to say goodnight, before George glitched again. Alex dropped the tablet onto the mattress. He put his hands behind his head, stared at the ceiling, and pretended it was a clean sheet of ice. There was nothing like the first few strides on fresh ice.

A knock on the door interrupted his daydreaming.

"Come in," Alex said.

The bedroom door inched open and light flooded in. It seemed brighter than it should have. Alex knew that wasn't good. Dad poked his head into view, then walked across the room and sat at the foot of the bed.

"Feeling better?" he asked.

"I'm feeling fine," Alex lied. "I was just mad."

"Because you got hurt?" Dad asked.

"Well…" Alex said. He debated whether to tell his dad what had really gone down, then decided not to. "Yeah, because I got hurt. Wouldn't you be mad about that?"

"I would be," Dad said. "Yes."

"*So*… there you go," Alex said, getting close to snapping.

"Your coach just called," Dad said, ignoring Alex's tone. "He wanted to know how you were."

"I said I'm feeling fine. Did you say that?"

"I said that you *said* you were feeling fine, but you probably weren't."

Why do parents know their kids so well?

"You don't know that for sure," Alex said.

"I used to play hockey, Son. I know what it's like to get your bell rung."

"So, what did the coach say when you said that?"

"He told me you shouldn't play tomorrow," Dad said. "We agreed that you probably shouldn't play for at least a week."

"That means my tryouts are over!" Alex said, his eyes becoming damp. "There are only two more skates before they make cuts."

He'd been doing so well. He would've done so well. Now he wouldn't get the chance.

"Yes, it does mean your tryouts are over." Dad smiled at Alex and patted him lightly on the shoulder as if he were an egg that might break. "Let's hope if that kid who hit you makes the team too, he treats his teammates better than just another kid at a tryout."

Just another kid, Alex thought. *More like just another* Native *kid.* These reflections distracted his foggy brain until suddenly the haze cleared.

"Wait a minute," Alex said, his misery washing away like rough ice underneath a Zamboni. "If that kid makes the team *too*, meaning... I *made* the team?!"

Dad chuckled. "Of course you made the team! Were you not at the same tryout I was?"

"I guess I felt good about some of the drills," Alex said sheepishly.

Dad stood up and went to the door.

Before closing it, he said, "I'm very proud of you, my boy."

"Ekosani, Dad," Alex said.

"Ekosi," Dad said.

CHAPTER 7

B Y THE DAY AFTER the hit, Alex was way less sore. Hour by hour, bright lights bothered him less and less. The only reason he wasn't playing was because everybody was being extra cautious, but he still went to the second and third tryouts. Alex told his dad he wanted to go because it would show the coaches that he was excited to be on the team.

"Sets a good example," Dad agreed.

As Alex watched, he guessed which kids he'd be playing with, who looked like they'd make it and who looked like they'd get cut. He noticed, too, that most of the kids were white.

Alex paid super close attention to two players. Wuerf, who had immediately come to check how Alex was doing when he arrived for the second tryout, was one of the best players on the ice. He was fast in a lumbering, determined kind of way and he was a grinder, winning almost every puck battle in the corner even though he was one of the smaller kids on the ice. He had awesome vision, too, making passes that even George might not have been able to make. Alex had no doubt he'd be playing with him this season, and he said as much to his dad, who was sitting beside Alex eating popcorn and drinking coffee.

"They're making two teams," Dad said. "So I hope he makes it *and* that he's on your team."

"For real?" Alex asked. "Two?"

Alex couldn't help but feel a bit let down, even if he'd only just met Aidan. He was the only player Alex had really made a connection with. Alex even thought Aidan might be the new George (not that George could be replaced).

"That's what I've heard from the parents," Dad said.

"Well, that sucks," Alex said.

"The Kodiaks and the Bruins," Dad went on.

"They couldn't think of anything except for bears?" Alex grumbled.

"Hey, at least neither of them has one of those Indigenous names, like the Natives or the Fighting Sioux or something," Dad said.

"I guess."

The other player Alex paid attention to was Terrence. He'd been made to sit out the second tryout as a consequence for the dirty hit but played in the third one. In Alex's opinion that was a pretty soft punishment. Alex learned that Terrence's nickname was Terry, which seemed like a stupid hockey name. It totally didn't fit him, either. Terry was something you'd name a teddy bear. And Terrence was definitely not a teddy bear, unless it was the kind of teddy bear that came to life and went on a rampage like in a horror movie.

The annoying thing was that Terrence was good. He was tough to get around on the ice, he was big, and he could skate backwards almost as fast as he could skate forwards. He made smart plays with the puck. More than anything, though, he could shoot a slapshot as hard as an adult. It was a real clapper.

Alex noticed Terrence's shooting ability during the last scrimmage before cuts. A player at the top of the circle took a shot on net, and the goalie redirected the puck into the corner. The winger got control of the puck, then slid it towards the blue line. Terrence moved the puck from his backhand to his forehand and teed it up. Three kids got out of the way when they saw that Terrence was about to shoot. The puck came off his stick like a bullet. It whipped through the air and was in the back of the net before the goalie moved. Alex was left with his mouth open.

"That kid can shoot," Alex's dad said, in the understatement of the year.

"You think?" Alex responded.

Terrence would be playing A1 this year, either with the Kodiaks or the Bruins. Alex hoped that whatever team Terrence was on, he was on the other one.

After the third tryout, every player was given a white envelope with a letter inside that revealed whether they'd made A1 or not. The players had to open the envelopes in the parking lot, in case somebody got upset and made a scene. Even though Alex knew he'd made the team, he felt nervous. Until he'd opened the envelope anything could happen. He hurried outside and tore it open with his dad watching expectantly. For a moment, the earth stopped spinning and everything went quiet. Alex pulled the paper out of the envelope, unfolded it, and read the letter.

THANKS FOR TRYING OUT! THIS YEAR YOU WILL BE PLAYING:

A1 ☑
A2 ☐

It was official. Alex performed a subtle fist pump, then gave his dad a low five. But the letter didn't say what team Alex would be playing on. When he asked his dad about that, he told Alex the coaches would have a draft. They would pick players, one coach then another, until all the players had been placed on a team.

Alex scanned the parking lot to see the other kids' reactions. He spotted Wuerf in the back seat of his mom's car. Even from a distance, Alex could see a big smile on his face.

"Wuerf made it," Alex said.

Dad laughed when he looked in Aidan's direction. "Not much of a poker face."

Next, almost against his will, Alex looked for Terrence. He found him standing by a minivan with his parents. He smiled while his mom hugged him and his dad ruffled his hair, like, "Way to go, Son." Alex didn't say anything about it, just shook his head. Great. There was a 50-50 chance they'd be teammates. Alex hoped the draft went the way he wanted it to: Aidan and him on one team, and Terrence on the other. That would mean he'd have to deal with Terrence's physical play, but only a couple of times a year.

Alex saw a mix of tears and smiles among the other players, along with parents who looked happy, proud, or angry. Some parents drove out of the parking lot calmly, while others peeled out like they were starting a drag race. Alex's dad was one of the calm parents. If Alex had not made the team, he would have left the parking lot the same way. Hockey parents could get fired up, but Alex's dad always kept his cool. That helped Alex keep his cool, too—for the most part.

As Alex's car passed Wuerf's on the way out of the parking lot, they waved at each other knowingly. As much as he didn't want to see Terrence, he hoped he'd get to see Aidan a whole lot more when the season began. At some point early in the week, they would get an email from the coaches letting them know what team they were on and when the first practice would be. It was less than a week away, but Alex knew it would feel like forever.

CHAPTER 8

THAT WEEK, as the night of the draft loomed, Alex's class took part in different activities leading up to the National Day for Truth and Reconciliation. They had guest speakers in their classroom, watched videos about the Indian residential school system, learned about smudging from an Elder, tied orange ribbons on the fence that surrounded the school, and finally, went on a field trip to the grounds of an old residential school in the city.

There were some differences from how Alex's school had recognized the day in Norway House. The kids there smudged all the time, so they weren't taught about it; they just did it. But honouring the children who survived, and the children who didn't, was the same. Alex thought about how in his community, most people had either lived through the history, or were directly connected to it.

Alex's kōkom and moshom had attended the Indian residential school in Norway House Cree Nation. His kōkom also attended Assiniboia Residential School, the destination of Alex's class field trip. Survivors were stationed in the field outside of the old building wearing bright orange shirts that read "Every Child Matters." The building was now the Canadian Centre for Child Protection. The place where kids like his kōkom had been hurt was now dedicated to protecting children.

An Elder told Alex's class about his experiences attending the school. They listened respectfully and carefully even though the story took almost an hour. It was hard for the kids to sit still for that long, even if they were outside on the grass. It was hard for Alex, because it made him think of his grandparents and what they had gone through. They'd never told Alex much about it, but he had heard enough. And sometimes, though they were almost always joyful, he saw it in their eyes. A bit of sadness that couldn't be hidden by a smile.

When Alex lined up to board the bus back to school, he was behind a boy named Thomas, who he sat near in class, and in front of a girl named Jennifer Neil, who he hadn't spoken to much. Jenny (she liked Jenny, not Jennifer) was one of the few white students in the school. She was nice to everybody. As they walked towards the bus, shuffling their feet as the line inched forward, she tapped Alex on the shoulder.

"Hi," Alex said.

At eleven, he'd never been all that interested in girls, but he knew Jenny was pretty and nice. Sometimes she made his cheeks feel warm.

"Hi." Jenny's eyes were wide and apologetic.

"Is everything okay?" he asked.

Jenny nodded.

"I was just wondering," she said slowly and carefully. "Did anybody in your family go to residential school? You're Indigenous, right?"

Alex didn't answer straight away. The words were in his mouth, on the tip of his tongue, but they refused to come out. He wanted to say that he was Indigenous and his grandparents went to residential school, but before he could say anything his mind went somewhere he didn't intend for it to go: To Terrence, bodychecking him during the first tryout. To Terrence, skating past him and saying, "Better watch where you're going, Chief." When his mind returned to the present, he answered Jenny with words that surprised him.

"I don't think I'm Indigenous," he said, and instantly felt ashamed for denying his culture. What was he worried about? That Jenny would hit him, too? "Not that I know of anyway."

"You don't *think* you are?" she asked, looking confused.

"Uh... I just don't know," he said, desperately wanting the moment to end. Now his cheeks felt warm for a totally different reason.

"Okay." Jenny nodded in a way that made Alex think she didn't believe him, but she didn't argue with him either.

All the kids boarded the bus and Alex sat alone. As the bus pulled out of the parking lot, he found himself staring at the old residential school wondering a million things. What had his kōkom really experienced there? How had it affected him? Why had he immediately thought of Terrence when Jenny asked him if he was Indigenous? Most importantly, why had he lied? The answer to all those questions came, against his will, in Terrence's voice, and in his words.

Better watch where you're going, Chief.

CHAPTER 9

FOR A FEW DAYS after the field trip, Alex felt like everything was influenced by having been called Chief. When he went to the corner store to get candy or pop, the clerk, a young white high-school kid, looked at him funny. It made Alex wonder if the kid might call him a name like Terrence had. One day, when he was playing outside with kids from the neighbourhood, it started to rain and puddles formed on the sidewalks and the street. The kids started to do what they called a rain dance and made war cries while they danced. Alex laughed, but it made him feel stupid.

In the middle of the week, Alex's dad finally got the email announcing the rosters. Alex was on the Kodiaks—and Terrence was going to be his teammate. It was as if Alex couldn't escape his presence.

"Oh no," Alex said.

All the other names seemed blurred out.

"What is it, Son?" Dad asked.

Alex pointed at Terrence's name. "That's the kid who hit me."

Dad sighed. "Well, you're going to have to get over that, if you're going to be teammates. Have you considered that maybe he didn't even mean to hit you?"

"He meant to, Dad."

"How can you be so sure?"

Alex opened his mouth, then closed it just as fast. If he mentioned anything about what Terrence had said, it would become an even bigger deal. Alex wanted it to magically go away.

"I guess I can't," he said.

"Give it a chance," Dad said, patting his shoulder.

When the initial shock of seeing that Terrence would be on the Kodiaks wore off, other names began to unblur themselves. The first name that jumped out at Alex was Aidan Wuerfel. The fact that Wuerf was on the team softened the blow of seeing Terrence's name.

Shortly after the rosters were announced, Alex was playing on his tablet when he got a chat notification. Somebody had already put together a group chat for the Kodiaks and added every single member of the team. Alex stayed up too late that night, hiding underneath his comforter so his parents wouldn't see the glow from his tablet if they came to check on him. He sent messages and random pictures to the rest of the team, as if they were already friends. It all felt normal and comfortable, and Terrence didn't say one bad thing to him. Maybe his dad was right.

At the 11A1 level, the coaches were still players' parents. The head coach for the Kodiaks was Ryan Johnston's dad, so Johnny had inside information on how the draft went down. He shared everything he knew with the team, even though his dad had told him not to. The top players drafted to the Kodiaks were Alex, Wuerf, Terrence, Johnny, and two kids named TJ and Huddy. Thanks to a kid named Cruiser, Alex became a topic of conversation because he'd been the first pick overall.

CRUISER: How was Robby picked 1st?

HUDDY: He hardly stepped on the ice, but…

WUERF: You saw him skate, right?

TJ: Exactly.

TERRENCE: Still.

JOHNNY: You just wanted it 2 b u, Terry.

TERRENCE: Whatever.

JOHNNY: He's good.

TERRENCE: Maybe they felt sorry for him.

HUDDY: That was dirty, dude.

ALEX: I'm literally right here.

When Alex joined the argument, the chat steered away from him and towards the team, the upcoming practice, and how they'd do this season. Before the chat died down at almost midnight, the consensus was that the Kodiaks would be a middle-of-the-pack team. A team called the Winterhawks were apparently going to be the best in the league by far. And middle of the pack or not, nobody could wait until the Kodiaks hit the ice for the first time, including Alex—even with Terrence on the team.

CHAPTER 10

WUERF AGREED TO MEET ALEX in the parking lot at Allard before their first practice. Alex's mom pulled up forty-five minutes before practice started, even though the players had been told to come half an hour early.

"You always need to be early," Mom had said. "You might've heard the term 'Indian time' before, that we're always late, but people don't know what they're talking about, or what time means to us."

The lot was already full. There must've been a practice before theirs, but Alex wasn't the only player on the Kodiaks who'd arrived early. He saw teammates he recognized from tryouts walking towards the arena from their cars. Other players were as eager to get onto the ice as he was.

"I guess everybody is on Indian time," he said under his breath as they found a spot at the back of the parking lot.

Mom laughed. "I guess so."

Alex and his mom happened to park beside Wuerf and *his* mom. When Wuerf saw Alex, he ran over and opened the door for him as if he were royalty.

"Thanks," Alex said, stepping outside.

"I'm not carrying your bag though," Wuerf said.

Alex got his own bag out of the trunk, and his Warrior stick. He walked with Wuerf towards the arena while their moms followed, getting to know one another.

In the lobby, parents were hanging out and younger siblings were running around playing tag or begging their parents for something from the canteen. Alex and Wuerf broke off from their mothers and, with popcorn crunching underfoot, made it through the crowd and entered the rink.

That's when Alex saw Terrence, and it made him feel instantly shaky.

Terrence placed his stick on the rack outside of the dressing room. He opened the door, but then looked around and met eyes with Alex. Alex's heart started to beat fast, and he stopped abruptly. He pretended to watch the kids on the ice. They were finishing their practice, doing a shootout for fun.

"You good?" Wuerf asked.

Alex's thoughts raced like skaters doing a speed drill. He'd avoided telling Jenny he was Indigenous, but telling Wuerf felt different. Maybe it was because Aidan could relate, in some way. They'd carried on their own chat since the roster was announced. Wuerf had shared with Alex that he was adopted. He just came out and said it, like it wasn't a big deal. Alex didn't think it was either. Wuerf sent Alex a photo of where his birth family was from, somewhere in Saskatchewan, and it encouraged Alex to send a picture of where he was from. It was a photograph of him in a boat near the shores of Little Playgreen Lake.

"Where's that?" Wuerf had texted.

"Home," Alex had replied after hesitating. "Norway House. It's a reserve."

He wondered if Aidan would make something of it, but he didn't.

"Oh, cool," he'd texted.

Alex's attention snapped back to the rink.

"You know I'm Cree, right?"

"Sure," Wuerf said. "I mean, I figured out that since you're from Norway House *Cree* Nation, you're probably Cree."

"I should call you Wuerf-lock Holmes," Alex said. It was the worst joke ever told. Wuerf grinned, but couldn't laugh, which Alex understood.

"I haven't told anybody else," Alex continued, pretending the joke had never happened. "Somebody might've guessed or thought I was, but..."

"Why don't you want people to know that?" Wuerf asked.

Alex watched the shootout competition for a minute, long enough to see two kids get stoned by the goalie. "What if my nickname becomes Chief, instead of Robby?"

"Terry was just being a jerk for some reason," Wuerf said. "Maybe he did that to try to look cool or something. He's never really hung out with the team. Kinda keeps to himself, I guess."

"Why?" Alex asked.

"Good question," Aidan said. "Not sure."

The buzzer blared, signalling the end of practice. It was time to get changed. Soon the Zamboni would start cleaning the ice. Despite his nervousness, Alex felt anchored by Aidan's presence. He placed his Warrior stick on the rack, and Wuerf placed his stick right beside Alex's, like their sticks were also going to be friends. Alex could hear the collision of boys' voices like rush-hour traffic on the other side of the dressing room door. Wuerf pushed open the door to reveal the team in various states of getting their hockey equipment on. Some kids were eagerly almost all the way dressed except for their helmets. Other kids had their shin pads on and that was it. Everyone was laughing and talking and looking as though they were having the time of their lives. They had spent two weeks worrying about making the team, and now that worry was over. Alex felt like he was the only one worrying about anything. He found a spot on the bench by the back wall with enough room for him and Wuerf. Alex saw Terrence on the other side of the room and did his best not to make eye contact.

When Coach walked in, the room went quiet in one second flat. He had eyes that were serious and kind. He looked like he might chew a player out for doing something wrong on the ice, but not in a mean way. Coach Kip—that's what he asked the team to call him—put his helmet on and greeted the team for the first time.

"Hello, Kodiaks," he said. "Some of you I've coached before and some of you I haven't, but we're all starting from scratch. You want the chance to try and win us a game late? To be on the power play? The penalty kill? You'll have to earn it. The harder you work, the more you'll get out of this season." He stopped in the middle of the room. "If everybody gives this team everything they have in the tank, we'll have a great year."

"What if we do that and still lose?" Johnny asked.

"Nobody's gonna beat the Winterhawks," Huddy added.

"If you think nobody's going to beat them, then they've already won the championship," Coach said. "We might as well give them the trophy right now and not even play the season."

Every player went silent.

"There are two things I want from you guys," Coach went on. "First, work as hard as you can every minute of every game. Can you do that?"

Coach was met with a chorus of nodding heads and yeses, some of them more emphatic than others, but Alex thought he was getting through to them.

"Good," Coach said. "The second thing is I want you all to have fun. But you know what?"

The room quieted one last time.

"I don't care if we lose as long as we try our best—but winning is pretty darn fun. Now who's ready to play some hockey?"

The dressing room erupted, and in that moment, the team suddenly felt like a team. One by one, the Kodiaks filed out of the room and into the rink, where they lined up at the gate to wait as the Zamboni cleaned the last stretch of ice. It drove out of the rink, leaving behind a gleaming sheet of ice and only a thin line of snow where the machine had exited. The Zamboni driver shovelled that snow away, and as soon as the doors clicked shut, the Kodiaks skated onto the ice for the first time that season.

CHAPTER 11

OACH KIP WASN'T JOKING when he said he wanted the kids to work hard. Alex thought the first practice might be easy, but he was wrong. It started off fine, with the team taking slow laps around the ice and shooting on Braxton, the goalie, while they did. Alex watched where he was in relation to Terrence at all times, making sure they were as far apart as could be. Terrence didn't seem to take much notice of him, except to throw Alex a glance now and again.

After a couple of minutes, Coach blew his whistle and started them off with a breakout drill. They hadn't done the drill more than a few times before Coach had them line up on the goal line. He didn't like how often they were missing passes and missing the net, so for the next ten minutes he made them skate until they could barely breathe.

Alex felt like he might puke and some of the other kids looked like they felt the same way, but nobody did. They ran the breakout drill a second time and did it better, almost cycling through the whole team before getting skated again. And that's how the practice went. They only got through three drills because whenever anybody messed up, everybody had to skate.

"You succeed as a team and you fail as a team," Coach said.

As a reward for their effort, Coach set up a shootout to end the super tough practice. Everyone lined up at centre ice with a puck on their stick, and one after the other they tried to score on Braxton. By the end of the first round, only three players had scored: Wuerf, Terrence, and Alex, who'd gone in with speed, faked backhand, and slid the puck through Braxton's five-hole.

The three remaining competitors lined up again, with Wuerf at the front, then Alex, and finally Terrence. It was the closest to Terrence Alex had been all practice. Being so close to him made Alex uncomfortable. He could almost feel Terrence's eyes burning into the back of his helmet.

Wuerf scored on his chance, then Alex skated in on Braxton, distracted by his own thoughts. He took a weak wrist shot that the goalie easily turned away, then took his place with the other Kodiaks along the boards. He watched Terrence skate to the top of the circle, tee up the puck, and rocket a slapshot off the crossbar and in.

After Terrence's puck hit the net, the buzzer rang as if it was signalling the goal. The Zamboni driver opened the doors, then climbed onto the machine and honked its horn to urge the kids off the ice. Coach Kip gathered everybody together by the gate.

"I just wanted to have a quick powwow to let you guys know that you did a great job today. With that attitude, we'll get better and better as the season goes on," Coach said. "I picked you guys for a reason, and we're going to have an awesome year."

After the short speech, all the coaches and players put a hand in the middle.

"Kodiaks on three!" Coach shouted. "One, two, three . . ."

"Kodiaks!" everybody shouted in unison.

Everyone left the ice pumped up despite being exhausted, bouncing on their skates towards the dressing room. Everyone except Alex. The word *powwow* kept echoing in his head. It felt like he'd been called Chief all over again. Alex had been to *actual* powwows on the rez, and he knew that what had just happened on the ice was not a powwow. They'd gathered for a pep talk. That was it.

The room was louder after practice than before. Music was blasting. Kids were tearing off equipment. Some of them were dancing around like they were at a concert. A garbage can in the middle of the room was a basketball hoop now. Player after player tried to throw their balled-up used sock tape into it. Some kids threw miniature snowballs they'd made from the flakes of ice on their skate blades.

Alex did not roll up his sock tape and shoot it into the garbage bin. He did not dance. He did not make snowballs from the ice on his skate blades. Wuerf tried to get him going when he noticed that Alex was quiet and detached, but Alex barely reacted. He was the first one out of the room, grabbing his Warrior stick on the way. Some of the parents said hi as he walked out of the building with his mom, but he didn't say anything in response. He did the same thing to them that he'd done to Wuerf: half-smiled and nodded. Alex had looked forward to practice for the last two days, but now he couldn't wait to get out of the building.

CHAPTER 12

ALEX STARED OUT THE WINDOW silently on the car ride home, lost in thought. His mom didn't bug him because she could tell he wasn't in a good mood. She usually held off for as long as she could before asking him what was wrong. What *was* wrong, anyway? He felt upset by the words people had used around him. Words that he just couldn't shake, no matter how hard he tried to let them go.

Chief.

Powwow.

Alex hadn't danced in a powwow before, but he loved watching the dancers and had always admired their beautiful regalia. He'd bought stuff from vendors, like food or music or, earlier this year, a beaded pin that looked like an orange shirt. He'd pinned it onto his shirt for the National Day for Truth and Reconciliation. Maybe that's why Jenny had asked if he was Indigenous.

Alex knew what the dances meant. The jingle dress dance, his favourite, was a healing dance. When he was younger, his moshom had told him the story of its origin. He still remembered it.

A long time ago, there was an Elder whose granddaughter got sick. When the Elder went to sleep, he had a dream about four women wearing jingle dresses and dancing a particular dance. A jingle dress has bells woven into the fabric, so that when you dance it makes a jingling sound. In the Elder's dream, the women showed him how to make dresses like theirs. They showed him the choreography of their dance and told him what song they danced to. After showing him all these things, they told him that if he did as he was taught, it would make his granddaughter well.

In the morning, the Elder woke up and immediately began to make a jingle dress. When he finished, he asked his granddaughter to put on the dress and taught her how to perform the dance. When she was ready, the Elder's entire tribe gathered together to watch her. Drummers sang the song the Elder had dreamed. When the girl started to dance, she could hardly stay on her feet because she was so sick. She had to be supported and carried by her people. But as the dance went on, she got stronger and stronger until she was able to dance on her own. When the drumming stopped, she was cured of her sickness.

There was meaning to every dance. There was meaning to a powwow. To Alex, the most important meaning was that it was a gathering. It meant community. When Coach brought the players together at the end of practice, calling it a powwow was wrong. It gave Alex a weird, confusing feeling.

Alex felt defensive of his community. There were so many things he loved about it, like the annual Treaty and York Boat Days, a celebration to relive his people's history during the fur trade, and to remember their will to succeed. Or small things, like how the lake looked in the morning, when the rising sun's light hit the ripples on the water. He wanted to shout it from the rooftops, but at the same time, he was worried about speaking up because Terrence had made fun of him, and Coach had treated an important ceremony like it wasn't important at all. Like it was just a quick meeting to discuss something. So, instead of shouting from the rooftop, he'd told Jenny he didn't even know if he was Indigenous.

"Is everything okay?" Mom asked. Her curiosity had gotten the best of her.

"I guess," he said.

"That's not convincing," Mom said. "You can talk to me."

"I know," he said.

There was another, shorter silence.

"A car ride is a good time to talk," Mom not-so-subtly hinted.

Could it hurt to say what was in his brain?

"Fine," Alex sighed, and told her what had happened at the end of practice.

Her first response was to click her tongue and shake her head.

"You know," she said, "sometimes people say things like that."

"Say things like what?" Alex asked. It was the first time he'd ever heard somebody say they were going to have a powwow unless they were actually going to have a powwow.

"They use words from an Indigenous culture in a way that's not what they actually mean," Mom said. "Like when somebody starts a new job and somebody else says they're the low man on the totem pole. They have no idea about totem poles. Like, why crest animals at the bottom aren't less important than the ones at the top."

"So are they just *trying* to be mean or..."

Alex's mind went directly to Terrence calling him Chief. Ever since then he'd thought Terrence was being a jerk, but did that mean Coach Kip was too?

"Not always," Mom said. "They can be, if they know it's wrong and still say it. Like when sports teams use mascots or names from Indigenous cultures even though they know it's offensive."

"Like that Washington team used to," Alex said.

"That's right," Mom said. "They say they're honouring us, but they know they aren't. It's just an excuse. But I think most of the time, people have gotten so used to saying things like 'let's have a powwow' that they don't think they're being offensive."

"What should I do when I hear people say something like that?" Alex asked.

"Well," Mom said, "if people don't know, then they don't know. And they *won't* know unless they're told." She glanced back at Alex and smiled. "The next time you hear something like that, and you know it's not okay, you should tell them. Anybody can educate anybody else if they know what they're talking about. I mean, who knows? Maybe if you say something, the person you say it to will educate somebody else. That's how these things work."

Alex nodded, but if it happened again, he didn't know if he could say something. Alex knew enough about powwows to educate Coach if he used that word in the future when he talked to the team. But if he said something, would his coach get mad at him? Would he think Alex was being disrespectful for correcting him? He was an adult, and Alex was a kid. Would it make things better? Was Alex brave enough to find out? In the end, Alex hoped those words, or anything like them, wouldn't come up again.

That would solve all his problems.

CHAPTER 13

THE KODIAKS' FIRST GAME was a week away and each practice was harder than the last. But Alex didn't care. He was on the ice playing the game he loved, and more than that, nobody said anything about powwows, nobody checked him and then called him Chief, and nobody asked him about his cultural background. The drills, the skating when they messed up, all of it became routine.

That all changed when it was time for everyone to choose their jersey numbers, and pick the team's captain and alternate captains. When all the players were dressed and ready to go, except for their helmets and sticks and gloves, Coach walked into the dressing room.

"Okay guys, it's time to choose who's going to be our captains this year," Coach Kip said. "Just remember, who you vote for sets the tone for the whole season."

He handed each player a pen and three slips of paper: one to vote for the captain and the others to vote for the alternates. Alex had no idea what to do. All he knew was that Wuerf should be a captain or an alternate and Terrence shouldn't be either one. Ultimately, he voted for Aidan as the captain, and Huddy and TJ as the alternates. He didn't think anybody would vote for him, except maybe Wuerf. Alex figured he would lead by example; he didn't need a letter on his jersey. After every player had made their choices, Coach Kip tallied the votes. The captain would be Johnny, and the alternates would be Wuerf and Huddy.

Coach Kip had decided they would choose jersey numbers alphabetically by last name.

"Aren't you worried somebody's going to choose your number?" Alex asked Wuerf, who would have to choose last.

Aidan shrugged.

"Everybody knows I'm 12," he said, pointing to the "12" sticker on the back of his helmet. "I've played with most of these guys, so they won't take it."

Alex hadn't played with any of the kids before, but everybody knew his number was 3. It was all over his stuff. It was on the practice jersey he wore, he'd written it on the Warrior after George gave it to him, and it was also on the back of his helmet.

The jerseys were hung on hooks on one side of the dressing room, from the lowest number (2) to the highest (35, which was already set aside for Braxton), and the kids were bunched together on the other side. Coach Kip went through the roster. When he called out a player's name, they went up and picked their number. Eventually, there was only one player before Alex, and so far, nobody had taken 3. He knew it wasn't a very popular number, but he liked it because his dad used to wear it.

Terrence got to pick right before Alex. His last name was Quick. He, like Alex and Wuerf and most everybody else on the team, had his number clearly marked on his equipment. It was even on his bag: 4. When Terrence went to choose his number, Alex wasn't worried at all. Alex watched as Terrence walked up to number 4. He put his hand on what should have been his jersey before letting it go, shuffling one step to the left, and picking number 3.

A collective gasp echoed through the dressing room. Even Coach looked at Terrence curiously.

"Are you sure about that, Terry?" Coach asked.

"Yeah, Coach," Terrence said. "I think it's time for a change."

Coach Kip looked at Alex, who felt like a deflated balloon, and shook his head with apologetic eyes. He gave Terrence one last chance to change his mind, but Terrence stuck to his choice. Alex surveyed the players who hadn't chosen yet to see what numbers they would take, based on their helmets and sticks and hockey bags. He took the only number that wouldn't upset anybody else.

That number was 4.

After practice, in the darkness of his bedroom, Alex made a video call to George. George could tell instantly that

Alex was having a bad day. It must have been written all over his face. And now that George was in front of him, Alex felt like he could let some of those emotions out. As soon as George answered, Alex's eyes welled up. They glistened in the glow of the tablet's blue light.

"What's going on, Robo?" George asked before even saying tansi.

"Nothing," Alex said. He went off camera for a second to wipe his eyes against his pillow. But when he put his face back in front of the screen, his eyes had already filled with tears again. He was a leaky faucet.

"Don't lie," George said.

Alex shook his head and the movement jarred some tears loose. There was no point saying nothing.

"What's my number?" Alex asked. He was one hundred percent sure George knew the answer.

"Three," George said. "Why?"

"Would you *ever* take somebody else's number if you knew that it was their number?" Alex asked.

"Never," George said. "I think I see where this is headed, though."

"You know that kid, Terrence, who called me Chief?" Alex asked, and this time he didn't wait for an answer to his obvious question. "He took my number!"

Saying it brought more tears. Saying it made Alex realize that Terrence taking his number was probably connected to Terrence calling him Chief. He was trying to upset Alex. The selection of a number had never been more offensive. Alex wiped away the tears again.

"Stop it," George said in disbelief. "He actually did?"

"I'm serious," Alex said.

"He's trying to mess with you," George said. "And it looks like it's working."

"You think?" Alex said. "I literally had to take his number!" Alex pictured himself wearing number 4. "I'm going to feel mad all the time wearing it."

"Or…" George began, but then stopped as if Alex should know what he was about to say. Like they were so close they could finish each other's sentences. Actually, sometimes they could, but not this time.

"Or what?" Alex asked.

"I'm just saying that he probably wanted you to get upset and stuff," George said.

"Yeah. I *am*. I guess he wins."

Alex gripped the sides of the tablet so hard that it was a wonder the screen didn't crack.

"So stop being mad," George said. "Be number 4 and play your best and don't let him win."

"But he's a jerk!" Alex said.

"He's a total jerk!" George said. "But it's just a number. My dad says that all the time. He says, 'Age is just a number.'"

"That's what old people say."

"Yeah. It's still true, though."

Alex took a deep breath, then exhaled all the air and tried to push the anger out with it. "I guess he wanted to tease me so much, now he doesn't get his favourite number either."

"Totally!" George said. "He'll feel so stupid if you don't make a big deal out of it."

Maybe there was a reason to like 4. Alex couldn't think of one now, but that didn't mean he wouldn't figure it out. He could always change the sticker on his helmet. He could erase the 3 on his Warrior and replace it with 4. Next year, if they were on the same team, Terrence might want 4 and Alex could keep it to get back at him.

"Thanks, George," Alex said.

After that, the two friends talked about other non-number-related hockey things. They talked about Norway House and stuff that was going on in the community. They talked about school. They talked about more hockey things. They talked about video games, like NHL, which was also a hockey thing. As time wore on, Alex's grip loosened on the tablet. By the time he got off the call with George an hour later, he was calm. He couldn't wait to get on the ice so Terrence could see how much he didn't care about wearing number 4.

CHAPTER 14

ALEX ALWAYS MADE SURE he kept as far away from Jenny as possible. If she was at the front of the room, he sat near the back. If she was close to the door, he sat by the windows. Alex didn't think Jenny made a habit of asking people about their cultural background, but he could sense that she knew he'd lied to her and didn't want to give her a chance to ask him about it. Avoiding her went just fine until one fateful recess. Alex was alone, stickhandling with a floor hockey stick and a tennis ball, when he heard her say, "Hi."

Alex had just "passed" the ball to the school's brick wall and looked up as it shot back towards him. It rolled across the concrete before stopping under Jenny's foot.

"Oh," Alex said, and everything in his body instantly felt unstable. "Hey."

Maybe it wasn't *only* that he thought she knew he'd lied. She'd just said hi and his heart was pounding.

"Did you know," Jenny said, "that when Tiger Woods was younger his dad used to distract him while he was putting?"

Alex leaned on his stick and tried his best to look cool, but he knew he didn't. He wondered if Jenny knew he was nervous, and that's why she'd asked a seemingly random question. It did make him feel a bit more relaxed.

"Why did his dad do that?" he asked. "I'm not a Tiger Woods expert."

"His dad knew one day he'd have to drain putts in front of millions of people, and what's more distracting than that?" Jenny asked.

"Okay," Alex said. "I get it."

Alex kept leaning on his stick and Jenny kept stepping on the ball. It was odd. It was fall, it was chilly out, but suddenly he felt very warm.

"I don't know much about golf. There's no golf course near…"

He'd been about to say there were no golf courses near Norway House, but if he told her that, she would know for sure he'd lied the other day about not being Cree.

"There's no golf course near…" she repeated, encouraging him to keep going.

"Near where I grew up," Alex said, which wasn't a lie. He did grow up in Norway House, and where he grew up there was no golf course. There was no golf course for, like, two hundred miles.

"Where *did* you grow up, anyway?" Jenny asked.

"Just some town up north." Alex hoped that would put a stop to her questions, and once again, he hadn't lied. Where Alex had lived in Norway House, in Rossville, was very much like a small town. "I guess you golf," he added, to help steer the conversation elsewhere.

"My mom takes me," she said. "I didn't like it at first but now I do. And I usually watch the final round of the majors. It's super calming watching golf. Especially the Masters."

Whatever that was.

"Why were you telling me about Tiger Woods?" he asked.

"Just seems like you need more practice with the whole distraction thing," Jenny said. "All I said was 'Hi' and you totally missed the ball."

She kicked the ball to him. Alex flipped his stick around in time to catch it on the blade, then began to stickhandle as expertly as he could.

"Want to try again?" Jenny asked, watching the ball move back and forth from his forehand to his backhand.

"Like, do I want to start passing the ball to myself again?" he asked.

"Yeah," she said. "I could throw stuff at you and see if you screw up."

"Throw stuff? Like, what kind of stuff?" he asked.

Jenny looked around. She picked up a pebble and tossed it at him. It hit him on the shoulder, which didn't hurt, but he still said "Ouch!" for effect.

"Oh, come on," she laughed.

"How about you count how many times I can pass the ball to myself before I make a mistake," he said.

"Wow, sounds like a blast," she said sarcastically, but she sat on the concrete, cross-legged, which Alex took as an invitation to continue passing the ball against the school. As he did, Jenny whispered, "One, two, three, four..."

"That actually makes me more nervous than throwing pebbles at me," he said.

"I can do both," she suggested.

Jenny picked up a pebble and prepared to throw it. Alex flinched and the ball rolled away. She laughed. She had an awesome laugh. He ran after the ball, caught it, then fired a long pass that hit the bricks and came right back to him. He received the ball perfectly, then stick-handled back to where he'd started before resuming the passing game.

Jenny started to count again.

"I have a game tonight so I'm practising, that's all," Alex said.

"Are you any good?" she asked.

"I think so," he said. "I mean, yeah. Probably. I'm not bad."

"Are you sure about that?" Jenny giggled.

She threw another pebble at Alex. This time, he didn't flinch.

"Yes," he said, trying to sound confident.

Jenny got up and brushed off her clothes just as the bell signalled the end of recess, as if she'd planned it that way. She smiled at him, then spun around and began to walk away.

"Well, good luck tonight," she said without looking back. "See you in class, Alex."

"Bye, Jenny," Alex said, after pausing for a few seconds to think of something to say that might sound cool. She probably didn't even hear him say bye. Before heading inside, he passed the ball to himself a few more times, imagining Jenny was still there throwing pebbles.

CHAPTER 15

THE KODIAKS were playing the Railcats in the first game of the season. Wuerf told Alex that the Railcats had finished in second place last year. They'd lost to the Winterhawks in the city finals. The Railcats were from Transcona, a big area of the city with lots of kids that play hockey, so they always had a strong team.

"Just like the Winterhawks," Wuerf explained as they walked through the parking lot towards the arena.

"Where are *their* kids from?" Alex asked.

"Like, so I live in St. James," Wuerf said. "The Kodiaks are all kids who live in St. James."

"Except for me," Alex said.

"And Terrence," Wuerf said.

"Terrence?" Alex asked.

"Pretty sure," Aidan said. "Although I don't think anybody's been to his house before. Anyway, the Winterhawks are from Charleswood *and* Tuxedo *and* River Heights and there are way more kids to choose from."

"Like Transcona," Alex said.

"Exactly," Wuerf said, as they walked through the lobby. "So, the Winterhawks and the Railcats are usually the best teams."

"What's a Railcat, anyway?" Alex asked.

Wuerf paused. Alex pushed open the door to the rink. They were met by a familiar and welcoming cool rush of wind.

"Well," Wuerf said, "there's lots of trains in that area, I think. And there must be lots of cats. I mean, there are lots of cats everywhere."

Alex laughed. There was no way the team was named after trains and cats. What were the Winterhawks named after? Hawks that flew in winter?

"Are there Kodiaks in St. James?" Alex asked, still laughing.

"I saw a coyote once near Assiniboine Park," Wuerf said.

"So we should be named the Coyotes then," Alex said.

He thought of his old team, the North Stars. He knew why they had that name. Constellations were important to his community. Most of the legends Alex had been told by his moshom involved the stars. Cree people in Manitoba mostly lived in the north, so the North Stars made sense. He supposed this was no different from the Winterhawks, if there were really hawks in their area that flew in the winter.

"The Coyotes suck," Wuerf said. "They literally used to be the Jets before the Jets left Winnipeg."

"I know," Alex said.

They placed their sticks on the rack, then opened the door and went into the dressing room.

"My dad is still mad about that, even though we have them back now," Wuerf said.

"Mine, too," Alex said. "I mean, I'm mad about it and I wasn't even born when it happened."

It felt like the Kodiaks were a professional hockey team. On each hook were two sets of jerseys for every player, one for home and one for away. Coach Kip was observant. Even though Wuerf was number 12 and Alex was 4 (which he was totally cool with!), their jerseys had been hung beside one another. And even though 3 and 4 were one after the other, he'd made sure Terrence and Alex were at opposite ends of the room.

It bugged Alex to see Terrence with 3, but he tried to stick to his plan of seeming perfectly content with his new number. Leading up to the game he'd made a list of reasons why it was good, to make the contentment more believable.

Four was an even number.

Bobby Orr wore number 4, and he was one of the best players of all time.

Rounded up from 3:30, 4 was the end of the school day.

That was a stretch.

Four was the only number that had the same number of letters as the value of the number.

That was also a stretch.

When all the players had gotten dressed, and the Zamboni was finishing its last lap around the rink, Coach dove into his pregame speech.

"On paper, we may not seem like the best team in the league," he said. "I'll be honest. There are more *talented* teams out there. We're going to lose some games and we're going to win some games. I want us to lose less and win more as the season goes on."

He'd been pacing back and forth but stopped in the middle of the dressing room.

"Do you know how we're going to do that?" he asked.

"We're going to work hard," Johnny said, the white C for captain bright against his blue jersey.

"That's right," Coach said. "We're going to work harder than anybody else. *Will* makes up for *skill*. Now are you guys ready to kick some butt?"

The players yelled "Yeah!" in unison.

"Kodiaks on three!" he said. "One, two, three…"

"Kodiaks!"

The starting lineup for the Kodiaks showed that Coach meant business. Wuerf was at centre, while Johnny and Alex were on the wings. Terrence and a kid named Joel, who was short but fast, were on defence. Alex had butterflies in his stomach. He glanced at the stands and saw his parents in the crowd.

"It's good to be nervous," his dad often said. "It gives you energy."

Alex had a whole bunch of energy, and he was ready to use it all up on the ice. The whistle blew, the ref dropped the puck, and the game was on.

Wuerf won the draw to Terrence, who slid it over to Joel. Alex crossed through the middle, and Joel hit him in stride. He shot the puck into the Railcats' zone off the boards, and Johnny retrieved it behind the net. He skated from one side to the other before passing it off to Wuerf in the corner. By then, Alex had skated into the slot, and Aidan slid the puck through a defender's legs right onto the tape. Alex snapped the puck on net but was robbed by the Railcats' goalie. With that whistle, the first shift was over. Alex, Wuerf, and Johnny skated to the bench, receiving a collection of fist bumps as they took their place at the back of the line.

That was as good as it got in the first period.

It was as if Alex's first shot woke the Railcats up. They dominated the rest of the period, firing shot after shot at Braxton, who did his best to keep the Kodiaks in the game. Near the end of the period Alex guessed the shots were probably around 1600 to 2. The only other shot the Kodiaks got was from Terrence, who'd taken a slap-shot from the blue line that the Railcats' goalie easily deflected into the corner.

When the buzzer sounded, the scoreboard read 3–0 for the bad guys.

There was a short break between periods, and Coach Kip had all the kids gather around him. (Alex was relieved that he didn't suggest they have another powwow.)

"Your effort isn't the problem," he said. "I know you're working hard, so you're not getting skated next practice for that. But you know what you *will* get skated for?"

Huddy put up a gloved hand and said, "They're just better than us, Coach."

Coach Kip let those words sit for a moment. He made eye contact with each of the kids, then shook his head.

"I told you before. They're more skilled than you, but that doesn't make them better. The difference right now is they're playing like a team. Look at how they're moving the puck in our zone. It's like they're on a power play."

There were so many times the Kodiaks could've done something productive if they'd worked as a team, but it was like everybody wanted to do it themselves. Alex knew he wasn't innocent. He counted two times when he could've passed the puck and didn't, then ended up turning it over. He decided that he was going to play better from that point on. To encourage his linemates, he gave them each a punch on the arm. Johnny and Wuerf nodded, like they'd been thinking the same thing.

It was still 3-0 when Alex and his line burst onto the ice for their first shift in the middle period. Joel flipped the puck so high in the air it almost hit an arena light before it landed deep in the Railcats' territory. Wuerf chased the Railcats' defenceman as he skated with the puck behind the net. He sent a desperate pass up the middle and Alex intercepted it. He had a clear shot at the net but saw Johnny in a better position. Alex wound up as if he were going to shoot, but when the goalie committed, he sent a crisp pass over to Johnny. He fired the puck into the back of the net for the Kodiaks' first goal of the year.

The rest of the period was back and forth. Every Kodiaks line picked up their game, but the score didn't change until late in the second frame. The Railcats dumped the puck into the Kodiaks' zone, and Terrence controlled it behind the net before stickhandling up the boards. He saw Alex waiting for a pass but looked him off and skated towards centre ice.

"What're you doing?" Alex called out, throwing his arms in the air.

He was wide open, and Terrence now had two Railcats players on him. One of them knocked the puck off

Terrence's stick, while the other went into the Kodiaks' zone all alone, took the pass, and buried it. Just like that it was 4-1. The Kodiaks were in as deep a hole as they were to start the period, despite having played way better hockey.

During intermission, Coach Kip stood behind the bench with his arms crossed. Sometimes silence says more than words. He was not happy. The first two periods were twelve minutes long and the third was fifteen minutes. There was time, but considering the score, it didn't feel like much.

When the third period started, the Kodiaks put on the pressure right away. It wasn't long before they'd drawn the first penalty of the game. Wuerf, Johnny, and Alex moved the puck back and forth between them as if they were playing a game of keep-away. When the puck went back to the blue line, Joel fired a slap pass to Alex, and he redirected the puck through the goalie's five-hole to make it 4-2.

On Alex's very next shift, with five minutes left in the game, he had the puck behind the net in the Railcats' zone. The goalie tracked the puck, hugging one post then the other while peering at Alex over his shoulder. Then Alex faked like he was going to make a move with his backhand, which caused the goalie to overcommit. Lightning fast, Alex pulled the puck to his forehand, stepped in front of the net, and slipped the puck between the post and the goalie's skate.

The score was 4-3.

With fifteen seconds left and the Kodiaks buzzing with their net empty, there was a faceoff deep in Railcats territory. Coach Kip asked for a thirty-second time out and drew up a play for the guys on the ice. Wuerf had to win the draw and pull the puck back to Alex, who would be lined up directly behind him. Wuerf and Johnny would charge the net, and Alex would have two choices: Fire a shot if he had a clear lane or draw the Railcats to him and pass to Terrence, who'd unleash a slapshot.

Both teams lined up for the faceoff. The ref blew the whistle. Wuerf choked up on his stick and got low to the ice. The puck was dropped, and Wuerf muscled it away from the Railcats' centre, getting it on Alex's stick as planned.

Everything moved in slow motion.

Wuerf and Johnny went to the net and the Railcats' defencemen collapsed, blocking a clear shot to the goal. The Railcats' centre and left winger raced toward Alex. Alex heard Terrence call for the puck. He looked at Terrence, whose stick was already raised high over the ice, ready to shoot. That was the play, Alex knew it, but his mind went back to Terrence not passing to *him*. Why should he pass to Terrence and let him be the hero? He'd hit Alex at tryouts. He'd called Alex Chief. He'd stolen Alex's number. All of this went through Alex's head in the moment he glanced in Terrence's direction. Alex looked away. He unleashed a wrist shot from the top of the circle. The puck sailed through the air, past the centreman and past Wuerf. The goalie had so much traffic in front of him that he didn't see it. He didn't even move.

Just as Alex was about to raise his arms in celebration, one of the Railcats' defencemen, the literal last line of defence, got his body in front of the shot. The puck hit him in the chest and fell harmlessly to the ice, a foot away from the goal line. The buzzer sounded for the final time, and the game ended.

The Kodiaks had come up short.

CHAPTER 16

ALEX WATCHED the Railcats hug each other and bump helmets with the goalie. It made him feel sick to his stomach. He looked at the puck, which was still exactly where it had landed. Not in the net. He replayed the moment a million times. Another inch to the side and the defenceman would have missed it. He knew the puck was heading right where he'd aimed. He should have shot it faster. He should have shot it harder. All of these "should haves" kept coming, but there was no time machine. The game was over.

It's just the first game of the season, he told himself before following his teammates to the other end of the ice, where they thanked Braxton for giving them a chance. A chance that Alex blew. The last "should have" popped into his brain when he saw Terrence in the crowd of players around their goalie.

He should have passed it to Terrence.

Maybe Terrence would have missed the net. Maybe the Railcats' goalie would have made the save. But Terrence had a clearer path and Alex knew it.

Terrence knew it, too.

On his way to line up and shake hands with the Railcats, Terrence spoke to Alex for the first time since the first tryout.

"Puck hog."

"You didn't pass it to me either!" Alex said.

Terrence was in front of Alex in line, and Alex wanted to trip him right there and watch him land on his face. He didn't though. He shook hands with every player on the other team, then skated towards the gate to get away from Terrence. He didn't want there to be another word between them. The worst thing about it was that Terrence was right. Alex *had* been a puck hog.

A lot of Kodiaks didn't place their sticks on the rack outside the dressing room, throwing them angrily on the floor instead. They landed in a heap like a game of pick-up-sticks. Alex placed his stick carefully on the rack. He wanted to throw it, but what if it broke? It was one of the only connections he still had to home, and to George.

Inside the dressing room the players were quiet, getting undressed with slumped body language. Alex met eyes with some of his teammates and half of them looked mad at him. Alex started to feel mad at them back. Without him they wouldn't have even had a chance to tie the game.

"Hey, don't worry about it," Wuerf said quietly. "Next time we'll kill them. We were down three goals."

"Yeah." Alex didn't say anything else.

Alex was the first to get changed and leave the dressing room, and he beat his parents out of the lobby and into the parking lot. He was walking so fast they could hardly keep up.

In the back seat of the car, Alex pressed his forehead against the window. It felt cold. It made him think of ice, then hockey, then the game. He may not have wanted to talk about it, but now he was thinking about it. He leaned forward, stuck his head into the front seat, and asked his dad how he thought he'd played.

Dad hesitated before saying, "I thought you played good."

Good was not good. Good was just okay. Just okay was not good enough for Alex. Alex was used to being great. If he'd scored that last goal, would it have been a great game? There was no question about that. Of course it would've been great.

But it wasn't.

Dad went on.

"I thought you made some good passes, had some nice shots, broke up some plays, and you got some points on the board," he said, as if he was a scout.

That was something Alex liked about his dad's analysis. He was specific and he was honest, which made it weird that he was avoiding the elephant in the room.

"What do you think I should have done?" Alex asked.

Dad shrugged, then asked a question to answer the question. "Why didn't you pass it over to that kid?"

Alex didn't hesitate. "That's the kid who hit me! And he didn't pass it to *me* when he should have, and the Railcats scored because of it."

"Take a breath, Son."

Alex took a deep breath and it calmed him.

"I didn't *want* to pass it to him," Alex said.

"Do you think the right play was to pass it to him?" Mom asked.

Alex didn't answer, which left time for Dad to make an observation.

"He's wearing your number," he said. "You didn't tell me that you didn't get number 3 this year."

"Yeah, well." Alex wasn't going to say anything about that, but it burst out of him. "Terrence's number is usually 4, but he picked right before me and chose 3 to make me mad."

"So you chose his number," Dad said.

"Everybody else had dibs on the other numbers," Alex said.

"Why didn't you take one of their numbers anyway?" Dad asked.

"I wouldn't have been a good teammate if I took one of their numbers," Alex said.

"Have all those kids been nice to you so far?" Mom asked.

"Mostly," Alex said, but realized he still hadn't spoken to many of his teammates, other than on the ice or in the group chat.

They turned onto their block.

"What have I told you about if somebody hits you on the ice, or punches you or trips you?" Dad asked. "If they do anything to you that you don't like."

"Don't do it back to them," Alex said. "But Dad ..."

He paused.

"What?" Dad said.

"Do you know why Terrence hit me in tryouts and took my number?" Alex didn't wait for his dad to respond. "He's racist! He called me Chief right after he hit me."

"You never told us that," Mom said.

"I'm telling you now!" Alex said.

"Well, I . . ." Mom paused. "It's just like when we talked about your coach saying 'powwow.' That boy may not have intended to say something racist. It doesn't make it right, but people have been conditioned to—"

"Talk about totem poles and powwows and all that crap, I know," Alex said, crossing his arms and leaning back into his seat. "So let's give them all a pass."

Or not pass *it to them at all*, Alex thought.

"That's not what I'm saying," Mom explained. "But have you talked to Terrence about what happened?"

"Why would I do that?" Alex asked. "I didn't do anything wrong. He should be the one to talk to me about it."

"Probably, but maybe you have to be the bigger person," Mom said.

"Dad!" Alex said, hoping to get a better answer out of him.

Dad took a long breath in, then let it out slowly.

"Your mother is right."

"Oh, great!" Alex threw his hands in the air. He gave up. "So I'm the bad guy!"

"Alex," Dad said calmly. "If this kid is going to be mean, don't retaliate. If it gets bad, or if he says something else, talk to him. If *that* doesn't work, talk to the coach. But when you're on the ice, you are all the same colour. Blue. Got it?"

They pulled up in front of their house. Alex got out of the car and slammed the door. He took his bag out of the trunk, carried it in through the side door, and slammed that, too. Once inside, he reached into his bag and started to throw everything onto the floor. His parents entered the house and watched him. Onto the floor went his shin pads, his jock, his elbow pads, his hockey pants. When he was done, his stuff made a big, stinky, messy pile. Alex stood there staring at it while his parents stood there staring at him. Then Dad reached into Alex's bag and took out the one thing left inside. Without a word, he handed Alex his blue-and-white Kodiaks jersey. Alex imagined the white bear roaring. He wanted to roar like that. Then he imagined each one of his teammates wearing their jersey.

Even Terrence.

"Okay," Alex said, taking a deep breath and letting it out slowly, like his dad. "I think I get it."

CHAPTER 17

ALEX KNEW he had to start playing differently. There was a week before the next game to think about how he could do that, and he started thinking about it as soon as he sat down for supper that very night. He hadn't taken more than two bites before he said, "I guess it would have felt way better to tie the game even if Terrence had been the one to score."

If Alex kept making good decisions, maybe at some point Terrence would do the same. *Lead by example.* Being selfish was not being a leader. The Kodiaks had two practices this week. Alex told his parents that starting at the next practice, he would feed Terrence so many pucks he'd be pooping rubber.

"Alex Robinson, that's gross," Mom said.

Alex laughed out loud.

"Don't go overboard," Dad said, trying not to laugh.

"Make the play if the play is there. If it's not, make a different play. You've got good instincts. Use them."

Alex liked his joke so much he repeated it to George that night. George dropped his phone and both boys laughed until they cried. When the laughing died down, Alex told George about the game.

"So the Warrior claimed its first victim," George said. "A-ho!"

"I guess so," Alex said. "Would've felt better if we won though."

"We lost when you were with the North Stars, too," George said.

"Yeah, but it's not the same, Cap," Alex said. "I didn't like some guys on our team and I still passed to them."

"They weren't racist though," George said.

Alex sighed. "I don't know if he's actually racist. He's probably just repeating what he heard somewhere else. Maybe from his parents or at school or..."

Alex was going to say from his friends, too, but he wasn't sure that Terrence had any close friends. He didn't seem to be buddies with anybody on the team.

"Like *you're* going to repeat your stupid joke?" George said.

"I already did, never mind," Alex said.

The boys suffered another laugh attack. It was just what Alex needed to cheer up, put the game behind him, and think about the next one.

The next day during afternoon recess, Alex went to the spot where he'd been when Jenny came to talk to him. He sat down where he'd been passing the ball off the wall so he'd be easy to find. He was tossing tiny rocks, one by one, pretending he was skipping them across the lake back home, when she sat beside him. She began to toss rocks with him.

"Hey," Alex said.

Whenever she was around, his palms got a little sweaty.

"Hey," Jenny said. "So, how'd your game go?"

"Oh, you know…" Alex said.

"Actually, I don't know, that's why I'm asking," Jenny said.

"We lost." Alex replayed the final seconds of the game and shook his head regretfully. Deciding to play different didn't erase the sting of losing. "By one stupid goal."

"That's so close!" Jenny said.

"I made a bad play." He picked up a pebble and threw it as far as he could. "That's why we lost."

"Oh." She threw her own pebble in the same direction as Alex.

"Yeah," he said. "'Oh' is right."

Alex threw a rock this time. It skipped all the way across the concrete and disappeared into the grass.

"Do you know what my mom says when we golf?" Jenny asked.

"No, what?" he asked.

"She tells me that when you take a bad shot you can't take it over again," Jenny said. "The only thing you can do is try to hit the next shot better."

"Try to learn from it," Alex said.

Jenny nodded, then threw a pebble. Alex threw one and tried to hit hers with it. It was a game Jenny didn't know they were playing.

"I bet you'd play way better if I came to watch," she said. "I could give you tips and stuff."

"What do you know about hockey?" Alex asked. "You golf."

"Don't hockey players golf?" she said. "I hear some of them golf all the time."

"That's after their season is over," he said.

"But still . . ."

They shared a silence that was kind of comfortable and kind of awkward. Alex kept glancing at her, looking away quickly when their eyes met.

"You really want to come to a game?" Alex said finally.

Jenny hit his rock with a perfectly accurate throw. She'd been playing after all.

"I don't know," she said. "Maybe."

Next practice, despite what Coach Kip had said during the game, he skated them hard. Alex thought this was probably because of what happened on the final play, and he felt responsible. They ran the same play repeatedly, to, as Coach said, "burn it into your brains." He wanted it to be automatic.

"Do you think about breathing or do you just breathe?" he asked.

"You just breathe," Johnny said.

"That's right," Coach said. "I want our breakouts to be the same way. I want you to do them without thinking." He made eye contact with Terrence. "Without trying to be a hero."

During the breakout drill, Coach rimmed the puck around the boards and Terrence stopped it with his skate blade, then gained control of it. He looked up, saw that the left side was blocked off, and skated out to the right, the side Alex was on. Terrence took a few long strides from behind the net. There was a moment when Alex wasn't sure what he'd do. But Terrence fired a crisp pass to Alex. Alex managed to corral the puck and redirect the pass towards Wuerf, who was open in the centre. They exited the zone efficiently. As Terrence and Alex skated past one another, Alex took a leap and nudged Terrence on the arm. "Nice pass," he said.

Terrence glanced at Alex. He didn't glare, didn't roll his eyes, didn't call him a name. He just gave a quick nod.

Next, they practised six on five, which was similar to their power play set-up. They spent a long time perfecting the last-second play, the same play that had gone so wrong in their loss to the Railcats. The first few times, when the puck came to Alex, the lane was clear and he was able to fire a shot on Braxton. On the last attempt, there was too much traffic in front. Alex moved the puck backhand to forehand, searching for a path. For a split second, he thought he had one, but the ending of the last game flashed into his mind. He glanced at Terrence, who was ready to take a slapshot, his eyes squarely on the black rubber disc. Alex faked a shot, then slid the puck to Terrence. Terrence didn't even try to control the puck. He one-timed it at the net, and it hit the mesh so hard that Braxton's water bottle jumped into the air. The six players on offence raised their arms as if they'd won an actual game. At the end of their celebration, Terrence skated over and gave Alex a fist bump.

"Nice pass, Robby."

"Nice shot, Terry."

CHAPTER 18

THE KODIAKS' SECOND game of the season was an away game at Jonathan Toews arena in St. Vital against the Knights. Before the puck dropped, Alex looked up at the stands and made eye contact with his mom and dad, who waved at him. He acknowledged them with a small wave, then scanned the crowd to see if Jenny had come. He didn't see her and felt let down, but shook it off. It wasn't like she was his girlfriend or anything. They hadn't talked about her coming again, after he gave her the time and place during recess last week.

From the start of the game, the Knights were under siege. By the middle of the first period, it was 2–0 for the Kodiaks and Alex had scored both goals. One of them was a power play marker that he roofed from the slot, and the other was off a three-on-one rush with him, Wuerf, and Joel, who'd jumped up into the play. TJ scored near the end of the first, so the score was 3–0 to start the second period.

The second period saw the Knights press back. The Kodiaks managed to score one goal, a redirection by Wuerf from Alex—his third point—but the Knights banged home three goals, two of them on the power play. The game had felt like it was going to be a blowout, but it turned into a close game: 4–3 to start the third. Coach Kip didn't like the Kodiaks' play in the second period.

"There's fifteen minutes to turn it around and play like you can play," he told the kids.

The message got through.

Within four minutes, the Kodiaks made it 5–3 on a goal from Huddy, and for the next ten minutes the Kodiaks didn't leave the Knights' zone. In the last minute, the Knights pulled their goalie to give themselves a six-on-five advantage. Terrence narrowly missed the empty net and iced the puck, which created a faceoff to the right of Braxton.

Off the draw, the Knights took a shot from the blue line that missed the net. The puck hit the back glass, where Terrence got control of it. Just when it looked as if he might take the puck up the ice himself, he slid it over to Alex. Alex stickhandled past one defender, then waited until he was over centre so that if he missed the empty net it wouldn't be icing. He was about to take a shot at the empty net, giving himself a hat trick, when he saw Terrence skating up the left side. He could hear his dad's voice: *When you're on the ice, you are all the same colour. Blue.* Alex passed it to Terrence and he scored, sealing a

6–3 win. When the buzzer sounded, the Kodiaks mobbed Braxton to celebrate, then Terrence skated over to Alex and tapped him on the shin with his stick.

"You could've had it, Chief," he said. "Thanks."

Alex felt a twinge at being called Chief again. He didn't like it, but he knew it meant something different this time around.

Alex shrugged. "You were open."

When the Kodiaks and Knights finished shaking hands, Alex and Terrence skated off the ice together.

"You're all right, Robby," Terrence said. "I thought you were all cocky at first."

"*That's* why you bodychecked me?" Alex asked. "You thought I was cocky?"

"It sounds stupid when you say it out loud."

Alex wanted to say it sounded stupid because it *was* stupid, but held his tongue. Terrence continued. "My parents gave me an earful on the way home after that, and I thought the coaches were going to cut me, to be honest. Especially when I had to sit out the second tryout."

"You would've been too good in A2. I'm glad they didn't," Alex admitted.

"Me too," Terrence said.

Alex didn't think he minded that Terrence was on his team anymore. Ever since the whole jersey number debacle, Terrence hadn't done much of anything to get under Alex's skin. Their silence during the first part of the season had grown out of the tension from that first tryout. It didn't have to be that way anymore. For the first time, Alex felt like Terrence was his teammate rather than his enemy. They weren't out of the woods, but at least they were on the path to somewhere better.

When Alex walked into the lobby after getting changed, he saw Jenny standing there. She was with her dad. Alex greeted her shyly. His face was flushed, but she would think it was because he'd been sweating during the game.

"Nice win," she said, giving him a fist bump. "You guys were awesome."

"Thanks for coming," Alex said. "I didn't see you at first."

"I had to see if my expert instruction helped out," she said. "I mean, come on!"

Jenny's dad told him he played a good game, then Alex thanked Jenny again before finding his parents and Wuerf's mom and Aidan. Aidan had watched the whole exchange between him and Jenny.

"I didn't know you had a girlfriend," Wuerf sang.

"Shut up! That's gross," Alex said.

"Spoken like somebody who has a girlfriend," Wuerf sang again.

"Next time we're on a rush I will not pass it to you," Alex said.

"Okay, okay, she's not your girlfriend," Aidan conceded.

Wuerf didn't mention Jenny again. All they talked about as they walked to their cars was the win and how they couldn't wait for the next game. How they couldn't wait for the rest of the season. Suddenly, it felt like the sky was the limit.

CHAPTER 19

THAT NIGHT, Alex chatted with George about the game, including his conversation with Terrence. They hadn't been talking long before the light flicked on, and Alex's dad walked in. Alex ended the call and tossed his tablet onto the bed.

"What's up?" he asked.

"It's 'Bring Your Kid to Work Day' on Monday," Dad said. "I was wondering if you wanted to come and see what I'm doing here in the city."

"Sure," Alex said.

Alex didn't hesitate, for two reasons. Reason one: Going to his dad's work for the day meant that he didn't have to go to school. The worst day of the school week was Monday. You got teased with two days of fun on the weekend, then boom. Math class. English class. Science class. Any class (except gym). Reason two: He was curious about what his dad did now. On the rez, he'd been a teacher. He was still involved in education, but Alex didn't know how exactly, other than he was doing something called administration. What did that even mean? Alex was about to find out.

On Monday, they pulled up in front of a door that had a symbol on it: an eagle with its wings wrapped around a medicine wheel that was divided into four sections coloured red, yellow, black, and white. The words beside the logo read First Nations Education Resource Centre.

"This doesn't look like a school," Alex said as he got out of the car.

"Well, it's not. It's more like a centre that *helps* schools get the things they need—specifically, First Nations schools," Dad said.

"Oh, administration and whatnot," Alex said. "Got it."

Dad laughed. "You'll get a better idea throughout the day. I help work on curriculum for schools that's created entirely by First Nations people."

"Is that important? To have it all made by First Nations people?" Alex asked.

They made their way down a hallway to an open area filled with cubicles and offices.

"It's very important," Dad said as they walked. "I grew up learning from curriculum that was made by people who didn't understand our history or our ways of living and learning. We have the right to develop our own curriculum for our own youth."

"Did my school have curriculum like that? I mean, the one back home?" Alex asked.

"It was a mix," Dad said. "We were... they are... working to get there. Change takes time."

"The school I go to now will never be like that," Alex said. If his family never moved back to Norway House, he'd miss out on going to a school that was meant for kids like him.

"You're right," Dad said. "But at least it's better than when I was young. People know a lot more now."

"What was the school like that you went to?" Alex asked. "Was it like the school moshom and kōkom went to?"

"I went to a day school," Dad said. "Day schools were pretty much like residential schools, only kids got to go home at night."

Alex followed his dad through a maze of cubicles to a door at the back of the room. When they stepped inside, Alex saw that Dad's office was bigger than Alex's bedroom. On one wall there was a map of all the First Nations communities in Manitoba with their traditional names, and on another wall, a fifty-five-inch television. Filing cabinets and bookshelves filled the rest of the space. There was a desk with a computer at one end of the room and a large round table in the middle. That's where Alex sat, and that's where he fell silent for a short while.

"What's on your mind, Son?" Dad asked.

"I just wish..." Alex tried to arrange his thoughts so the words coming out of his mouth made sense. "I've heard a lot of stuff about Indigenous people since we moved here—and most of it isn't good. Like, we're lazy and poor and we all live in the North End. I know none of that is true, but I wish people could see *this*, you know?"

"First of all," Dad said, "there is absolutely nothing wrong with living in the North End."

"People say it's dangerous and a bunch of other stuff," Alex said.

"I wonder if those people ever spent time in the North End or met people who live there," Dad said.

"I don't know," Alex said. "Probably not."

"Second of all," Dad said, "you have to know that there are Indigenous people who are struggling. We're lucky that we're not, but a lot of our people are. Some of us are on social assistance. Some of us are addicted to substances."

"So why do we live in a house and you have a job, and other... I mean, some of us don't?" Alex asked.

"A lot of bad things have happened to Indigenous people in this country," Dad explained. "Whether it's at the Indian residential schools, or during the Sixties Scoop, or how we get treated differently in hospitals or by police. Sometimes, all the things we've been through are hard to deal with. And if there aren't supports to help us, we might do unhealthy things to try to feel better."

"Why is it just us who has to deal with all of this?" Alex asked.

"It's not just us," Dad said. "But it *is* a problem, in the city and in our communities." He swivelled his chair around and looked at the map from top to bottom. He was quiet for a while, like Alex had been. Eventually, he turned to face him. "If the roles were reversed, if settlers, for example, had to go through what we went through as a people, they would be in the same position that many Indigenous people are in today. Do you know what that means?"

"No," Alex said.

"It means that even though we're different from each other, even though Indigenous people are different from settlers or Black people or whoever..." He sighed. "We're all humans first. We can all struggle. We can all treat each other badly. But we can also try to be better, and to do better for ourselves."

Alex ran his hands through his hair. He thought of what happened with Terry, the bad and the good. Terrence had treated Alex badly, and, in turn, Alex had treated him badly. But they were trying to be better, too.

"So, why did you come to work *here*? I mean, is it because of what you just told me?"

"I think so," Dad said. "But also, the government cut funding to on-reserve education. I offered to leave my position so others wouldn't have to lose their jobs. I knew people down here in the city who worked here, and they offered me a position when they heard I wasn't going to work at the school on the rez anymore."

"So you took it," Alex said, and he couldn't help but wonder what his life would be like now, where he would be, if his dad hadn't offered to get laid off. Playing with George on the North Stars, gunning for another championship. Alex voiced this to his dad.

"Well, you know what you have to do then, right?" Dad said.

"What's that?" Alex asked.

"You have to win a championship down here," Dad said matter-of-factly.

"Just like that," Alex said.

"Nothing's easy if you want to do things in a good way," Dad said.

He got up and searched through the books on his bookshelf. He placed a stack on the table in front of Alex.

"What's this?" Alex asked.

"You didn't think you were going to sit here and draw or watch cartoons all day, did you?" Dad asked.

Alex stared at the books. There were some textbooks, some picture books, and some chapter books. He saw that all of them were about Indigenous people.

"I never had books like that when I was a kid," Dad said, sitting down at his desk.

"So, what do you want me to do with them?" Alex asked.

Dad chuckled. "I have some things to get done, so I want you to read for a little while until I have work for you to do."

Alex checked out the covers and the titles. There were books by Julie Flett, Monique Gray Smith, Christine Day, Beatrice Mosionier, Chelsea Vowel, Richard Van Camp, Nicola Campbell, Brett Huson, Cherie Dimaline, Richard Wagamese, Katherena Vermette, and Tomson Highway. Alex randomly picked one by Julie Flett and started reading. It was about the Cree language. Alex knew a bit of Cree, but he'd always wanted to be fluent, like his dad. Seeing his language, Swampy Cree, made him feel proud.

Alex read while his dad answered a never-ending flood of messages. At mid-morning break, Dad brought him to the lunchroom, which was filled with people. Most of the staff were Indigenous. Dad said he worked with people from many different cultures: Cree, Anishinaabe, Dakota, Dene, Métis, Inuit, and more. Some of the staff were non-Indigenous.

Everybody seemed to get along. Alex felt comfortable there. He hadn't been around this many Indigenous people since they'd left Norway House. But it wasn't just the familiarity of being around other Indigenous people. Everybody in the lunchroom was working hard and doing good things for schools in First Nations communities. Alex worked hard, too, just at hockey. They were good at what they did, and he was good at what he did. They weren't worried about what other people thought, so he shouldn't be either.

After the break, Alex had to do actual office work for the rest of the morning, but Alex's dad said he could take the books home to read later. He filed paper after paper in the cabinets lined up along the wall in his dad's office. They had lunch, then went into a meeting that lasted the rest of the day.

On the way home, they went to a drive-thru and sat in the car eating burgers and fries.

With his mouth full of food, Dad said, "That wasn't so bad, was it?"

Alex swallowed a big bite of hamburger.

"Nope, not so bad at all."

It wasn't just "not so bad." It was one of the better days he'd had since moving to Winnipeg. His mind was whirling with all the people he'd met and everything he'd learned.

"I can't wait to tell Mom all about it," Alex told his dad.

Dad quickly finished the French fries he'd stuffed into his mouth. "Maybe don't tell her we ate fast food twice today, though."

CHAPTER 20

THE AUTUMN PASSED QUICKLY. Unfortunately, the Kodiaks' first win wasn't the beginning of a huge run of dominance. Coach Kip said the kids got too confident. The next game, the Kodiaks played a team that was worse than the Knights and lost badly. That dipped them below .500 and they fell to the bottom half of the league. The next game was better, but they lost that one as well. Then there came a tie, a win, and a few more losses, and that's how things continued.

It was a roller-coaster ride.

Alex's experience of being Cree in the city had its up and downs, too. Alex liked who he was, but it was hard not to get upset when other people *didn't* like him. And for no reason—only because he was Native. During one game, a kid on the other team called Alex a "savage" after he took a penalty for slashing. Then, a couple of games later, after Alex scored a goal, an opposing player said his shot was like a "tomahawk chop." When remarks like that came racing at him, he couldn't help but feel frustrated by some kids' racist attitudes.

Still, for the most part, Alex continued to have a good year. Through the first twenty games, he had thirty goals and fifteen assists. Wuerf was Alex's mirror image on the stats sheet. The linemates were leading the team in points, followed by Johnny and Terrence.

Coach caught Wuerf and Alex checking the stats online for their league, finding their names on the list of scoring leaders. He'd taken the phone from Aidan and showed them the standings instead. The Kodiaks were fourth last, with a record of 7-10-3. The Railcats were in second place with only two losses, and the Winterhawks hadn't lost a game. Nobody believed they could be caught, but the Kodiaks' focus was on trying to get good enough to compete with them in the playoffs.

One day, Coach gave the kids a speech about their underachievement. He wasn't upset that they had a losing record; he was upset because they were capable of being better, if they worked harder and executed what they practised.

"I told you at the beginning of the year that all I wanted was for you to work your hardest. Can any of you really say you've given it your all, every game?"

Crickets.

"If you're satisfied with losing when there's no excuse to lose, then keep doing what you're doing. If you're happy to be the low man on the totem pole, keep putting in 70 percent effort, not 100 percent. But if you want to do the best you can, you need to give everything you have on the ice."

In the dressing room, Alex was quiet for a different reason than his teammates. They were quiet because Coach was not happy with how they were playing. Alex was quiet because Coach had made the totem pole comment, something his mom had talked about earlier in the year. It was almost as if she was preparing him to hear it, like it was inevitable.

While the other players changed, Alex stayed in his equipment. He looked at his stick, where the name Warrior seemed bolder and brighter than ever before. People thought being an Indigenous warrior meant something it didn't, that it meant "savage Indians" scalping people or shooting arrows. But Alex knew warriors almost always fought for their people and against things that weren't right.

Enough was enough.

Alex got up from the bench with his skates and gear still on. He walked across the dressing room and out the door while his teammates watched him curiously. He went one room over, to the coach's room, and knocked.

"Come in," one of the coaches said, his voice muffled through the door.

Alex took a deep breath before entering the room. The coaches had their skates off and bags packed, ready to go but just sitting around. Alex's heart was beating fast and his palms were sweating. He wanted to leave, but instead cleared his throat and leaned on his Warrior stick as if it could support not only his body but his confidence in what he wanted to say.

"What's going on, Robby?" Coach Kip asked.

Alex looked down to the floor in response. "Uhhh..."

"You can look at me," Coach said. "I'm not mad."

"It's not that," Alex said, without explaining, as he continued to look down.

Alex had read lots of books about different Indigenous cultures, including their cultural traits. Some traits that he'd heard after moving to the city were false, like being lazy. He went to school and played hockey and read and played outside with kids in the neighbourhood, and almost never sat around doing nothing except when he played NHL with his friends. But everybody could be lazy. That wasn't exclusive to Indigenous people. Some traits were accurate in a funny way that made a light bulb go off in Alex's head like, "Oh yeah, I *do* do that." The funny ones were things like lip pointing. He'd seen his mom and dad do that, and he caught himself doing it from time to time.

Another trait he'd learned from his mom was that some Indigenous people did not make eye contact as a sign of respect, especially for authority. He'd learned that the hard way when he got in trouble with his teacher at the beginning of the year. Like then, Alex wasn't consciously avoiding eye contact with his coach. Alex respected Coach Kip even if he'd said a few things that bothered him.

"Alex?" Coach said.

Alex forced himself to look up, but how could he say what he wanted to say?

"It's nothing really," Alex said quietly. "It's just that ..."

He looked down again, noticed he'd done it, and tried to look up. He glanced at Coach Kip, then away from him.

"It's just that what?" Coach asked.

"Well, when you say stuff like 'let's have a powwow' or 'low man on the totem pole,' I don't think it's really... good. Like it doesn't make me feel good."

Coach Kip looked genuinely taken aback.

"Alex," Coach said, "I didn't even think about those things before I said them. They just came out, like figures of speech. We say them and don't give them any thought, you know?"

"I know that, but it feels like you're making fun of Indigenous people even if you don't mean to be," Alex said.

His hands were shaking. His knees were too. In fact, his whole body was trembling. He'd never been so nervous in his life. When Coach didn't answer straight away, Alex continued, because it was so quiet. The silence made him feel worried.

"We don't even have totem poles," Alex said. "I mean Cree people. But totem poles, where Indigenous people *do* use them... well, it's not bad to be at the bottom anyway." Alex grasped his Warrior stick even harder, but talked quieter. "So being the low man on the totem pole isn't really awful. I don't think."

"I'm guessing powwows aren't pep talks at a hockey rink either, are they?" Coach asked.

"Not exactly," Alex said. "People dance different kinds of dances in different kinds of regalia and the whole community comes out and..." Alex remembered the last time he'd gone to a powwow with his family, then controlled his excitement and brought himself back to the present. "Anyway... there's powwows in my community, but not in a hockey rink."

Coach Kip leaned forward, elbows on his knees, and looked at Alex. Then he reached out and gave him a light, encouraging punch on the arm. He looked around the room, meeting eyes with the other coaches, and Alex did the same. None of the coaches looked annoyed or upset.

"I'm glad you told me," Coach said, "and I'm sorry I made those comments. Honestly, I'm sure I'll mess up at some point in the future, but tell me if I do, okay? And don't feel nervous about it."

Alex let out a long breath he'd been holding in.

"Okay, Coach."

"It took courage to do that," Coach said. "That's the sort of courage I want to see from you on the ice more often, too. Deal?"

"Deal," Alex said.

He left the room feeling better and thought he might be able to do something like that again. Maybe he'd even talk to Terrence about what he'd said. When Alex walked into the dressing room most of the kids were gone, and soon enough, as he took off his equipment and put on his clothes, he was alone. But he didn't really feel that way.

CHAPTER 21

WHEN CHRISTMAS CAME AROUND, Alex was supposed to have a couple of weeks off with no games or practices. He was looking forward to that. The Kodiaks had been clawing their way up the standings, Coach had been skating them hard, and everybody was tired. Alex couldn't wait to play shinny at the outdoor rink. No stress. Hockey in its purest form. But a day into the break, his parents got a call from Norway House Cree Nation. They wanted Alex to play for the North Stars in the Winter Indigenous Cup, a tournament held in one of the nicest rinks in Winnipeg: the Hockey For All Centre. A ton of Indigenous kids and parents from all kinds of First Nations communities would be there.

"It'll be like an urban reserve," Dad told him.

"Would you like to play?" Mom asked.

Once his family had moved away, Alex thought he'd never get to play with the North Stars again, but here was his chance. More than anything else, he'd be reunited with George. He'd get to see his best friend in real life. Not just at hockey, either. George would stay at their house for the week.

"Yes!" Alex said.

Who needed a break anyway?

It was awesome having George around. When he got to the city a day before their first game, they hung out together in Alex's room, doing what they'd done every night since Alex had moved: talking until late about anything and everything. The reception was way better in person.

Alex asked Jenny if she wanted to come watch a game. At first, he just said that he was in a tournament at the Hockey For All Centre, but Jenny did what she did best: asked him a bunch of questions. He either had to lie or tell the truth. He realized he was ready to be honest.

"The Kodiaks are in a tournament?" she'd asked.

"No, not exactly," he'd said.

"Not exactly? They either are or they aren't."

"Okay, they aren't. I'm playing for another team."

"What other team?" she asked.

"They're called the North Stars. They're from Norway House. That's my reserve."

"I *knew* you were Indigenous." Jenny punched him in the arm.

"Is that okay?"

"Of course it's okay. Is it okay that I'm white?"

"Yeah."

"Well then, it's okay that you're Indigenous, silly."

Alex felt like a weight had been lifted off his shoulders. So, Jenny came to Alex's games until she went down south with her family for the rest of the Christmas break. She said watching hockey was better than watching golf. She even said she liked watching him better than watching Tiger Woods. Alex liked that he could talk sports with her. He liked that she didn't annoy him, which girls could do. Sure, she made him nervous sometimes, but he kind of liked that, too.

Other non-Indigenous people were also watching Alex's games. Aidan came to a few, and Alex was glad to see some of his other teammates. When news of the tournament and Alex's ice times hit the Kodiaks' team chat, he hadn't expected to see anybody. Alex thought he played better than normal when some of the Kodiaks were in the stands. When he won player of the game not once, but twice, he knew he wasn't imagining it.

The Norway House Cree Nation North Stars were the kings of the Indigenous hockey teams in Manitoba—that was a fact. They were the defending champs. The Winnipeg team was pretty good, though. It was made up of non-Status Indigenous players, most of them Métis and some who were First Nations but not registered band members. The out-of-province teams were deadly. The teams from Saskatchewan were particularly awesome. The playoff draw gave the North Stars a path to the final without having to play any of them, so they managed to get there without much trouble. Cross Lake did give them a scare in the semifinal, at least until the third period, but

Alex scored a natural hat trick to end the game, sending his teammates into a frenzy.

The North Stars won second place. The Big Spirit Cree Nation Eagles from Saskatchewan were too good. The North Stars gave them a run, and it was a tie game with ten minutes to go in the third, but they ended up losing 6-4, including an empty net goal.

"Those don't really count," George consoled Alex after the game. "It was really 5-4, to be honest."

Winning a trophy with the North Stars would've made the week perfect, but even with the loss, it was pretty good.

Alex was sad to see George go. They'd spent the entire week together, joined at the hip, making up for lost time. But Alex knew they'd be right back to video chatting every night. He couldn't wait for the sun to dip the day George left so he could call him up and talk. He couldn't wait for it almost as much as he couldn't wait for the second half of the Kodiaks' season.

You could only take a break for so long, and when the Kodiaks had their first practice after two weeks off, he could tell everybody else felt the same way. It was their best practice of the year. It made him think that maybe the Kodiaks could do to the Winterhawks what the North Stars couldn't do to the Eagles.

CHAPTER 22

I N JANUARY, the 11A1 league held its all-star game. By
then, the Kodiaks had reached .500 for the first time
since the beginning of the season. Alex was selected
by the Kodiaks' coaching staff, along with Wuerf, Terrence, and Braxton. The game was held at Allard. It
seemed like all the important games were held at Allard.
The playoffs would be there, too.

The all-star game was a weekend-long event, with a
skills competition on Saturday and an actual game on
Sunday. Kids were separated into the same two teams
for both days, depending on their area of the city. The
skills competition included the fastest skater, the best
passer, the best puck control, and the most accurate shot.
All of the players got to compete in a breakaway competition, which would also decide the winning goalie for the
day. Alex was chosen for the fastest skater and the most
accurate shot, while Wuerf would be in the stickhandling

and passing competitions. Terrence was competing in the most accurate shot.

Alex thought that he should do well in his events, but didn't think he was a shoo-in to win. There were so many good players, especially from the top two teams.

He made it to the final of the fastest skater competition, where he went up against a winger from the Winterhawks named Jackson. Jackson, tall and broad-shouldered, had breezed into the final. As Alex and Wuerf watched him from the bench, Wuerf said Jackson had long strides. He took one stride when most of the other kids took two.

"I don't think you're going to beat him," Wuerf said as Alex skated onto the ice.

After a moment of annoyance, Alex grinned. All year, Wuerf had told it like it was, and Alex appreciated it. He was telling it like it was now, so what was there to be annoyed about? He was right, too. Both players did one lap around the rink at the same time, starting at opposite sides, and Alex crossed the finish line half a second slower than Jackson.

"Nice try," Jackson said as he skated past Alex after the race.

Alex couldn't tell if Jackson was being serious. He sounded sarcastic. But rather than start something with the Winterhawks' star, Alex just said, "Thanks," and left it at that.

Alex thought he'd have a much better chance at winning the most accurate shooter. He'd scored lots of goals from that position. There were five targets set up in the net: one at each corner and one in the middle. When it was Alex's turn, Wuerf and Terrence gave him a pat on the back, then Alex began to skate towards the net.

On the way, he heard Jackson say, "Good luck," and this time it was *for sure* sarcastic.

Alex ignored him.

Then Jackson added, "Pretend like you're shooting your bow and arrow."

Alex stopped and faced the bench. Jackson and some of the players around him were laughing. Lots of things went through Alex's mind in the few seconds he stood there. His first thought was, *Did he really say what I think he said?* His next thought was, *That's super ignorant to say I use a bow and arrow because I'm Indigenous.* Alex let it bother him so much that he only hit three targets and didn't make it to the next round.

The breakaway was a simple event. Every player had a turn, and the ones who scored moved on to the next round. On and on it would go until there was one shooter left from each team. They'd keep shooting until one kid scored and the other missed.

Alex used a favourite breakaway move on his first turn, going in with speed on the forehand, moving the puck to the opposite side of the blade to fake a backhand shot, then switching to his forehand once more. He scored easily, and not many kids could say the same. Braxton and the Railcats' goalie were brick walls, and by the end of the third round there were only two kids left: Park, the best player on the Winterhawks, and Alex.

The stands were full, and everybody was going crazy.

Park went first. He skated in on Braxton, smooth and fast, and just when he seemed about to deke to the left, he wristed the puck towards the top right corner of the net. Braxton reached with his trapper but couldn't get to it. If it had been a perfect shot, the puck would've gone in. But it rang off the crossbar, dropping onto the ice at the goal line. The ref dramatically signalled "no goal" by waving his arms side to side over and over again.

Alex was next. He skated towards centre ice, giving Park a tap on the shin pads as they passed each other. The puck was waiting for him, perfectly placed in the centre dot so that it looked like a pupil surrounded by a red iris. Alex's heart was thumping and his hands were shaking. He took a deep breath, then skated towards the other blue line. When he hit the blue line, he turned back towards centre ice and built up a head of speed, ready to charge in on the goalie. Just as he was about to pick up the puck, he heard a war cry, or what a kid must have thought a war cry sounded like.

It stopped Alex dead in his tracks.

He quickly saw where the sound had come from: the other team's bench. Some kids were laughing, some were snickering, and some were looking away like they didn't want any part of it. Jackson's glove was off and his cage was raised so he could make the sound by fanning his hand over his mouth.

Alex opened his mouth to say something, but before he could, Terrence called out, "Hey, don't be a jerk!"

"Oh yeah?" Jackson said, still laughing. "Or you'll do what?"

"Next time we're on the ice together I'll take a slapshot right at your stupid head, that's what," Terrence said.

Jackson knew Terrence meant it because he shut up after that, securing his cage onto his helmet and moving out of sight of the Kodiaks' big defenceman.

Alex felt confused. He and Terry had been getting along for a while now, but Terrence calling Alex Chief wasn't that different from what Jackson had done today. And now Terrence was sticking up for Alex? He didn't know what to make of it. At that moment, Terrence met eyes with Alex.

"Go win this thing," Terrence said.

That sounded like a good plan.

Alex stood over the puck at centre ice, closed his eyes, and took another deep breath. He opened his eyes and burst forward with the puck, crossed the blue line, and went in on goal. The goalie glided away from the net towards Alex, stopping at the top of the goal crease. He was a big goalie, and from Alex's position, there wasn't much daylight. With his body, Alex made a motion like he was going to deke left. The goalie tensed for less than a second, but Alex knew that he'd been frozen. Alex leaned forward, pressed down on the ice with his stick so that it bent like a banana, then snapped a shot. The puck flew like a perfectly thrown football and zipped past the goalie's glove, pushing back the mesh.

Alex skated past the net at full speed then turned sharply around with his arms raised. His teammates flooded off the bench and mobbed him in the corner, and he could hear parents on the other side of the boards applauding by slamming their hands against the glass.

Eventually, the Zamboni driver steered the machine onto the ice and broke up the celebration. One by one, the players dispersed. Alex was joined by Terrence as he headed off the ice to the dressing room. When they were on solid, rubber-matted ground, Alex pulled Terrence's shoulder, asking him to stop.

"Thanks for doing that," Alex said, breaking a short silence.

"No problem," Terrence said, and paused. It was probably only for a few seconds, but it felt like minutes. Then, while avoiding eye contact, he added, "Maybe now we're even. You know, for before."

"Hey," Alex said, giving Terrence a light punch on the arm. "You thought I was cocky, remember?"

"That's not a good excuse and you know it," Terrence said, but Alex saw the hint of a smile that Terry couldn't really hide.

"We can't go back and change it," Alex said. "We can only do something different next time."

"Yeah," Terrence said. "I guess."

Alex took a deep breath. He knew that if they were really going to be teammates and put the past behind them, he needed to say something he'd been thinking about for a while, no matter how awkward it was.

"Can I tell you something?" Alex asked. "Speaking of doing things different."

"Sure," Terrence said.

"Okay, so..." Alex started, took another deep breath for courage, then kept going. "I don't think it's good to call me Chief. It's kind of just as bad as what Jackson was doing, even if you didn't mean it like that."

Terrence's shoulders dropped. Alex didn't want to make him feel bad. "A lot of people probably don't know that," he added.

"I've heard other people say that. I had no idea it wasn't okay," Terrence admitted. "I won't do it again."

"Cool," Alex said. "Robby is way better than Chief anyways."

The Zamboni rumbled past them, leaving behind steam and a trail of fresh ice, but not before the driver called out, "Way to go, boys!"

"I'm glad you told me about the Chief thing and all that," Terrence said. "I live near the Arlington Bridge, and there are Indigenous families in my neighbourhood. I'd feel so stupid if I said something like that to any of them."

"Hey! *I* live near there!" Alex said. "Like, in the West End. That's close to you, right?"

"Yeah," Terrence said. "I didn't know you lived there."

"You never asked."

They shared a brief silence, but it wasn't exactly uncomfortable. It was like they were both processing everything that had happened, from when they'd first met to now.

"So . . . we're good?" Terrence asked.

"We're good," Alex said.

Then, in the hockey version of a bro hug, Terrence gave Alex a rap on the arm and Alex punched Terrence lightly on the chest. As though kickstarted by the exchange, the boys turned and, together, began walking to the dressing room.

Alex's team lost the all-star game the next day by a big margin, but he still felt like he'd won. Not because he won the breakaway competition on Saturday, or even scored two goals during the game itself. But all that stuff with Terrence? It was over. There'd be no more bodychecks and no more bad names thrown his way, accidental or on purpose. Alex knew that for sure when Jackson didn't say a thing to him all game. Each time he looked like he wanted to, Jackson would glance over at Terrence, and there he was, shaking his head as if to say, "Don't even try it."

"If Terrence told me not to do something, I wouldn't either," Wuerf remarked.

"Nobody wants a puck to the head," Alex pointed out.

"Not from Terry anyway," Wuerf replied.

"You'd have no head left at all," Alex said, which threw him, Wuerf, and Terry into a fit of laughter.

CHAPTER 23

THERE WERE ONLY TWELVE GAMES left in the season. The Kodiaks weren't in jeopardy of finishing near the bottom of the standings, but they needed to finish as high as possible to get an easy first-round opponent in the playoffs. Coach Kip said playing a weaker team would get their feet wet, adding, however, that they should never count on an easy win. The team was practising more often, and Alex felt like all he did was go to school and play hockey.

He spent time with his friends when he had a spare moment.

He hung out with Jenny a lot. During outdoor recess, they tobogganed or had snowball fights or built forts or skated on the makeshift rink. When it was too cold to go outside, which happened a lot in Winnipeg, they played Pokémon (sometimes just trading cards back and forth) or basketball or mini-sticks. They sat next to each other in class. They were pretty much inseparable. When Alex played NHL before bed, he played online with Jenny or Wuerf, or on the best nights, with Jenny *and* Wuerf.

Alex and George exchanged play-by-plays of all their games. George kept Alex up to date on all the happenings in Norway House and asked if Alex had broken the Warrior stick yet. Alex had not. There was only a nick on the heel that didn't affect anything. Alex taped it up to make sure the sliver didn't get bigger.

"It needs to last at least until the end of the season," Alex said.

"Don't take any big slapshots," George said.

"Don't worry about that," Alex said, "I suck at slapshots."

Alex went over to Terrence's place a couple of times. Terrence told Alex he was embarrassed about where he lived, but Alex didn't see why. It was nicer than the bungalow he and his family had lived in on the rez, and he didn't think his home in Norway House was bad. They played video games, including NHL, and Terrence even started to join Alex, Wuerf, and Jenny when they played online. For NHL, Alex and Terrence made characters that had their skills and looked like them (if they were ten years older).

Alex turned twelve years old in February, a few weeks after the all-star game. The Kodiaks were on an awesome winning streak that had started before the all-star game and continued throughout the month. They climbed well above .500 and into the top five in the league. Alex didn't do anything big for his birthday, just had his friends over— the ones he'd made since moving to Winnipeg: Aidan,

Jenny, and Terrence. They played video games and watched a movie and played street hockey and ate cake.

After the party, Alex felt like even though Norway House Cree Nation was his home IRL, Winnipeg could be a home, too. Everything was finally in place. He missed George and he missed home, and that would probably never change, but he could visit whenever he wanted as long as he didn't miss hockey or school.

Alex had teammates he really liked, and after a few months of uncertainty, they seemed to like him, too. The Kodiaks weren't the North Stars, but they didn't have to be. His friends accepted him for who he was. It wasn't a big deal to them that he was Cree. It made him feel dumb for having spent a chunk of the season worrying what other people would say about his identity, but at least he didn't feel dumb now. And the more he read the books his dad brought home, the less dumb he felt. The better he felt about where he was, the better he played on the ice, and the better his team did. So much so that when the regular season was over, the Kodiaks were in fourth place. They'd crawled all the way out of the bottom of the league and were now one of the teams to beat. Nobody wanted to play them.

The playoffs were just around the corner, and everybody was pumped.

CHAPTER 24

THE PLAYOFF FORMAT was confusing to Alex. In his old league, the playoffs were straightforward: the top team played the last team, the second-place team played the second-last team, and on it went. If you lost, you were out. If you won, you kept going. The series were best of three, and the final was best of five.

Simple.

It made sense that things were more confusing here. The city was more confusing in general. On the rez, the directions were like, "Head down this road until the end, then turn right, and when you see the school bus, that's the house." In the city, there were so many streets and traffic lights and cars and it never calmed down.

Aidan helped Alex understand how the playoffs worked. The bottom line was, if you wanted to win the championship, you had to keep winning games.

But here's the detailed version.

If you got to the final, the series was a best-of-three, but until then, you advanced to the next round by winning just one game. If you happened to lose, however, it didn't mean your season was over. Every team was guaranteed at least two games. Wuerf called it a double knockout. The top two teams—the Winterhawks and the Railcats, of course—got byes into the second round. If you didn't lose, you only played four games until you made it to the final. If you lost and were sent to the B-side, you had to win seven in a row to climb all the way back to the final.

"But there's no B-side final or anything?" Alex asked.

"Nah. There's only one final, and a third-place game for whoever loses in the semifinals," Aidan explained.

"So you don't want to be on the B-side," Alex said.

"Right," Wuerf said. "But it would be worse to be on no side at all."

With the hot streak the Kodiaks were on, and with the Railcats and the Winterhawks getting byes, they were starting the playoffs near the top of the league. They were playing the Twins, a weak team they'd beaten four times during the regular season. None of those games had been close. The kids were confident, but at the end of the last practice before playoffs, with the players huddled together in what he did *not* call a powwow, Coach Kip said, "Never look ahead. Always look at what's right in front of you."

Anybody could beat anybody in one game. In a longer series, the Twins couldn't have won. The Kodiaks were faster, scored more, and had a better goalie and bigger defencemen. They were stronger in every category. But if they had one bad game, who knew what could happen?

"You need to get your feet wet," Coach said, "but be careful not to drown."

The playoffs started on Saturday afternoon, and the arena was packed. It felt like an NHL playoff game. Alex couldn't believe how many people were stuffed into the lobby. There were a lot of kids running around and causing havoc, but mostly there were parents and grand-parents. The adults waiting for kids who'd just finished their game looked happy or upset depending on if their kid's team had lost or won. Those who were waiting for the next game to start looked nervous. Even Kodiaks parents looked nervous. They weren't looking ahead to the second round either.

Alex and Wuerf shouldered their way through the crowd. There was hardly enough room to breathe. As they slowly moved forward, he felt a tug on his shoulder. He turned to find Jenny with her mom, both dressed in blue clothing.

"Are you ready for the big game?" Jenny asked.

She had to shout over the volume of the lobby. Alex had to shout back.

"Yeah!" he said. "I think so."

"Is it lame to wear Kodiaks colours?" she asked. "I thought it would be like the White Out, only a Blue Out."

When the Winnipeg Jets made the playoffs, all their fans wore white. It looked cool on television. Alex did a quick scan of the lobby and found that most of the Kodiaks fans were wearing the same shade of blue. He thought it would look awesome when they were together in the stands.

"If it was lame, you'd be the only one," Alex said. "Actually, it still wouldn't be lame even then."

"I feel like I've become a super fan, so I should look the part," Jenny said.

"Thanks for coming," Alex said.

"Of course!" Jenny said.

Aidan pulled him away.

"I have to steal our boy," Wuerf said.

"I better go," Alex said.

"Good luck!" Jenny said to Alex and Wuerf.

"We don't need luck!" Wuerf said.

The boys made it to the end of the lobby and entered the rink.

"Coach said not to be cocky about the game," Alex pointed out to Wuerf.

"I'm not," Wuerf said unconvincingly.

During the regular season, players showed up at different times. Some kids came early and some kids came late. Alex and Aidan were usually among the first ones there, but today they walked into a full dressing room. They were the last to arrive, thanks to being held up by Jenny (although Alex didn't mind getting held up by Jenny). Coach Kip looked like he minded, as he sarcastically thanked them for coming. Once they sat down, he went over the game plan. It boiled down to playing smart, including making smart mistakes—mistakes that didn't lead to chances for the other team.

"Let's keep up the momentum from the second half of the season," Coach said.

If the Kodiaks won, their next game would be on Wednesday after school. If they lost, they would play tomorrow evening on the B-side. Nobody wanted to play tomorrow. Getting a few days off between games meant extra days to practise.

In the rink, the electric atmosphere was impossible not to notice. It wasn't just the packed stands. It was the posters that parents had taped to the glass with messages of encouragement for their team. It was the never-ending applause the moment the players skated onto the ice. It was the music blaring from the speakers. It was the coolness in the air. All of it sent shivers across Alex's body. He could feel the hairs on his arms stick up under his equipment.

The warm-up had an urgency to it. The Kodiaks did two hard laps, then got right into a drill meant to get the puck on their sticks and shake off the jitters. Two forwards skated to the red line from either side of the ice, crossed each other between the blue line and centre ice, then went in on a two-on-one. Nobody really tried to score. Braxton needed to feel the puck on his pads as much as the players needed to feel the puck on their sticks.

When it was Alex's turn, he sprinted up the boards to centre ice and began to turn towards the puck. Suddenly, something took out his leg. He fell forward and his cage hit the ice. Hard. As he lay flat on the ice, he turned his head to see a player from the other team getting up. The two had collided with each other. Alex got to his feet and skated over to the other player.

"Sorry," Alex said, extending his glove.

The kid fist-bumped him and said, "It's all good."

The opponents parted ways, but as Alex skated off, he heard somebody in the stands yell, "That Native kid slew-footed my son!"

Alex turned to see who it was, but there were so many people, there was no way he was going to figure it out. He shook his head and kept skating.

The rest of the warm-up went by in a blur. Before Alex knew it, he was leaning on his stick at the edge of the circle, ready for the puck to drop.

He took a deep breath. Nerves were good but not a crazy amount of nerves.

The ref looked to his right. He looked to his left. He made sure both goalies were ready. The crowd kept cheering. The puck dropped and the game was on.

CHAPTER 25

THE TWINS CAME TO PLAY. Nobody had told *them* they were supposed to lose. Or maybe the pressure was off *because* they were supposed to lose, so they just played hockey. Whatever the reason, it totally showed in the first period. The Twins had the Kodiaks back on their heels.

There was no score after ten minutes, but it could have been 4–0 if not for Braxton. At the ten-minute mark, Alex got caught flat-footed and reached with his stick as a winger skated past him. The Warrior got stuck in the winger's legs and he fell to the ice. The ref immediately threw up his hand, and Alex went off on a tripping penalty.

The puck didn't leave the Kodiaks' zone during the power play, and with twenty seconds left in Alex's penalty, the Twins scored. The Kodiaks were down 1–0. Alex stayed in the penalty box for a moment longer than he had to. He looked up at the score and tried not to feel down about it, even though he knew he was responsible for the goal.

There were two periods left.

There was lots of time.

Alex tried to ignore the Twins' fans slamming on the glass as he left the penalty box. But then he wondered if parents were doing the slamming. His mom and dad would never taunt a twelve-year-old kid. He glanced back, and sure enough, it was adults. *What the heck?* Alex shook his head and kept skating. When he got back to the bench, Aidan patted him on the shoulder along with a few other teammates.

"Move your feet, Robby," Coach Kip said. Then as if he'd read Alex's mind, he added, "There's plenty of time left, boys. Let's play our game."

When the second period started, the Kodiaks decided they'd start playing hockey. Right from the opening faceoff, they spent most of their time in the offensive zone, firing shot after shot at the Twins' goalie. After five minutes they still hadn't managed to get one by him, but Coach kept saying that as soon as they scored one, they'd get a bunch more. They just needed to stay patient.

"I hope we don't get goalied," Alex said to Wuerf as they sat on the bench, waiting for their turn on the ice.

On the very next shift, everything changed. For once the puck was in the Kodiaks' zone, because the other team had dumped it in to relieve pressure and make a line change. Alex looked up ice and saw a lane. Terrence had the puck behind the net and Alex sprinted to get it.

"Terry, leave it!" he called.

Terrence skated away, pretending to have the puck. Alex gathered it in full stride and came out from behind the net at top speed. He carried the puck up the right side and easily deked around the winger, who'd just come onto the ice and wasn't ready to match Alex's quickness. The same thing happened with the centre. He tried to angle Alex out by rubbing him into the boards, but Alex squeaked by. He immediately knocked the puck off the boards to get around the defenceman, the last person who could stop Alex—and Johnny, who'd busted in on the left side. Alex gave Johnny a good look to sell a potential pass, but he didn't have any intention of getting rid of the puck. At the top of the circle, Alex snapped a shot over the goalie's shoulder.

The Kodiaks' fans exploded. Alex raised his arms and was mobbed by his teammates. After the ref broke up their celebration, Alex skated to the bench. The Twins' fans had been stunned into silence by Alex's end-to-end rush, and some of them were giving him nasty looks. He was so pumped up that, instead of ignoring them, he turned to face the crowd and smiled, raising his arm with a finger pointed in the air.

It was like Coach said. After they scored once, the floodgates opened. On Alex's next shift, he went down on a three-on-one with Aidan and Johnny. This time, instead of using Johnny as a decoy, the kids played tic-tac-toe, making the defenceman look silly, and Alex tapped the puck into an empty net after the goalie got turned around. The Kodiaks had taken the lead, and their fans were getting louder and louder.

Alex and the four other players on the ice celebrated again. Alex skated towards the bench flanked by his teammates, which felt like protection against any nasty looks from Twins parents. He focused straight ahead, but there were a few shouts even louder than the Kodiaks' cheers.

"Way to get a ringer!"

"Go back to where you came from!"

Alex kept his head down until he heard his mom yell at the other parents.

"He's more from here than you are!"

A fan shouted back, "Oh, I guess we're all settlers, right?"

The argument continued as Alex took his place on the bench. He did his best to block out what he'd heard, and what he was still hearing.

Aidan put his arm around him and said, "Don't worry about those jerks."

"I bet half the people here are thinking the same thing," he said.

"*We* aren't," Terrence said.

Coach Kip waved the ref over, and they talked for a few minutes before the game restarted. Alex tried to hear what they were saying but couldn't. He got a good idea, though, when the ref skated over to talk to the timekeeper. Finally, the timekeeper, who doubled as the announcer, got on the mic.

Barely audible over the shouting and hollering from the stands, the timekeeper said, "If there are more outbursts like that, anybody caught saying something inappropriate will be asked to leave the venue."

The warning was met with a mix of cheers and boos, but when those died down, the crowd remained quiet. Everybody focused on playing hockey once more.

Near the end of the second period, the Twins took a penalty for hooking, and the Kodiaks, who had all the momentum, went on the power play. The Kodiaks spent the first half in the Twins' zone. They moved the puck back and forth from one side of the ice to the other so fast that their opponents looked dizzy. With a minute left in the power play, Alex took a snapshot on net. It hit the goalie in the chest and he smothered the puck, forcing a faceoff. Alex and his linemates skated towards the bench, but Coach motioned for them to stay on, so they lined up again in the Twins' zone.

Alex stood opposite a winger named Gill, who'd been shadowing him most of the game. In the first period, Gill had done a good job. In the second period, not so much. Alex glanced to his right, and he could see the frustration on Gill's face. It was dripping from him like sweat. Gill must've noticed Alex looking at him, because he turned his head and locked eyes with Alex. Gill opened his mouth, hesitated, looked to the stands as if for motivation, then said, "Dirty Indian."

Alex felt like he'd been punched in the stomach. He forgot about hockey. What Gill said to him, along with the parents in the stands, was too much. He couldn't take it anymore. He didn't just forget about hockey, either. He forgot about the trip to his dad's work, the books he'd been reading, telling Jenny he was Cree, talking to the coaches about totem poles and powwows, mending fences with Terrence, all of it. All the good stuff went out, and all the bad stuff barged in with anger so hot Alex felt as though he might spontaneously combust.

He straightened up and faced Gill, who did the same. Somewhere deep down, Alex knew what Gill was trying to do. He knew what the parents were trying to do. If they couldn't beat Alex and the Kodiaks fair and square, they were going to resort to calling him racist names. *Was winning that important?* Alex dropped his Warrior stick, and it took a lot of willpower not to drop his gloves too. He knew if he did he would be playing into their expectations of him. They'd call him a savage.

"What did you say to me?" Alex asked.

"You . . . you heard me," Gill said.

"Take it back!" Alex said.

"You're just a dirty Indian," Gill repeated, even though his voice was a bit shaky. "My dad says so."

At that, Alex lunged at Gill with both gloves extended and knocked him to the ice. Gill cried out in pain and writhed dramatically. Alex was sure he didn't hit him that hard, but he also knew that he shouldn't have hit him at all. A ref skated over and held Alex back. A linesman stepped between Alex and Gill as if Alex might try to push him again.

And there was the crowd. Alex was sure the parents on the Kodiaks' side had been shocked into silence—nobody on the team had done anything like this all year. But the other side was shouting and booing at Alex. All Alex wanted to do was get out of there. He wanted to get off the ice, out of the arena, and as far away from the game as he could.

He got his wish.

Seconds after he pushed Gill, the head referee looked Alex dead in the eye and said, "You're out of here!"

Alex should have been upset. He probably was upset under all the other emotions. But mostly, he was relieved. He was given two minutes for roughing and a ten-minute game misconduct, which meant that his game was over. The other kid got nothing. Alex skated to the gate, glancing back as he left the ice.

Some of his teammates, the ones on the bench who hadn't heard what Gill said to him, looked mad at him for losing his cool. Coach Kip wasn't arguing the call. Players on the other team were pleased, and why wouldn't they be? The Kodiaks' best player had been thrown out, and it was only a one-goal game.

Alex had been called names and yet *he* was the bad guy. He slammed the gate and stomped into the dressing room, slamming that door behind him too.

The game wasn't over, but it was for Alex. And the worst part was, he didn't care.

CHAPTER 26

"I NEVER WANTED TO COME HERE ANYWAY!" Alex shouted in the dressing room, to nobody but himself.

His heart was racing faster than it did when he was playing. He took off his equipment piece by piece, throwing everything into his hockey bag as hard as he could. After he put his clothes on, he sat and simmered for a couple of minutes, and while he did the game went on. He could hear the fans cheering or groaning or gasping. But not booing anymore. There was nobody to boo since he'd been kicked out of the game.

As much as Alex told himself he didn't care, he wondered what was going on. But he managed to ignore his curiosity. He slung his bag over his shoulder, left the room, picked up his stick, and walked out of the rink without checking the score. As he passed the stands, he heard a couple of Twins' parents talking about him under their breath.

"There he goes."

"Back to the reservation."

I'd love to go to the rez, he thought. He wanted to shout it out loud.

Instead, Alex pushed through the doors and into the lobby to find his parents waiting there. When he saw them, all the emotions he'd been feeling turned to tears. He tossed his bag onto the floor at their feet and sat between them. They put their arms around him and he sobbed, burying his face in his hands.

Alex cried for several minutes, until his parents told him they should leave before the game was over and fans flooded into the lobby. He guessed they were worried about the other parents, who clearly hated him, seeing him there in the open. Alex was in no condition to handle that. His dad took his bag, Alex grabbed his stick, and they walked outside to the car. His mom turned on the ignition and they sat in silence as the car warmed up, the hum of the engine the only thing that dared make a sound.

"I didn't mean to push that kid," Alex said after a while.

If he didn't say anything, nobody was going to say anything. He was sure his parents were waiting for him to explain himself. He could only imagine how upset they were at him.

"When you drop something and it breaks, you meant to break it," Mom said.

As if she hadn't been clear enough, Dad added, "You meant to push him."

"Well, he deserved it," Alex grumbled.

"Maybe he did," Mom said. "But it wasn't up to you to punish him for whatever it was he said."

"He called me a dirty Indian!" Alex's tears had subsided, but now they came back in full force. "And that wasn't the first time I got called a name today."

When his parents didn't respond, he took a deep breath, then glanced at his mom and dad. They looked genuinely taken aback. His dad's lips were pursed. When he was mad, his dad pursed his lips. He never, ever shouted. Lips could do lots of things, more than just point. Alex's parents exchanged a look.

"Okay, he did deserve it," Dad said. Alex thought that if Gill was a grown-up and his dad was in Alex's place, his dad would've decked the guy. Without shouting, of course. "But that's what the refs are there for."

"The refs didn't do anything!" Alex said. "They kicked *me* out, not him!"

"They should've kicked him out, and those parents too," Mom said sternly. "Did they know what he said to you?"

"I don't know," Alex admitted. "They were there right after I pushed him. Maybe they just saw me push him and that's it."

"We have to believe that authorities, refs or police or whoever, will do the right thing. That's why they have the jobs that they have," Dad said, his lips now relaxed.

"Yeah, and what about when they don't do their job?" Alex asked. "Nobody just pushes somebody for no reason. They didn't even ask me what happened!"

"They were probably..." Mom sighed. "Oh, I don't know."

"There are better ways to deal with it than violence," Dad said. "He said words, you pushed him. That's not right, Son."

"You'll always have to deal with people treating you differently because of who you are," Mom said. "That's the history of this country. It doesn't mean you have to be okay with it, or do nothing about it, but there are better things to do. That's what your father is saying."

She had a point, of course. And she'd demonstrated it herself, when she spoke up after those parents had shouted at Alex from the stands. The engine continued to hum. The car kept heating up. Alex wiped away tears. He found a spot in the back seat to stare at and didn't move his eyes from it.

"Do you remember that march we went to last year?" Dad asked.

Alex remembered everything about it. The bodies of Indigenous children, children who'd attended Indian residential schools, had been found in unmarked graves. Too many people to count came together to honour the children, to say that what happened wasn't right and demand action. Most of all, Alex remembered how the march was about Indigenous people and how they've been treated, but more than just Indigenous people were marching. There were people of all different cultures and ages and gender identities and everything. He bet that nobody who was in the stands today had been at that march. At least, not on the side of the Twins.

"I remember," Alex said.

"There are better things to do, and there are better people out there who will help you do things in a good way," Dad said.

"It's just that sometimes bad people are the loudest," Mom said.

"Like all those stupid fans," Alex said.

"Some people can be jerks, but you just have to go out there and play hockey and focus on the people who appreciate you for who you are," Dad said.

Alex turned to face the arena. Nobody had left the building yet, but the game had to be over by now. Soon, everybody would come outside.

"Can we go?" he asked.

"Sure, honey," Mom said. "We can go."

On their way out of the parking lot, all the way to the road, Alex didn't take his eyes off the rink. When they turned onto the street and began to drive away, the front doors opened and people filed outside. It was too late to tell what had happened.

CHAPTER 27

EVERYBODY ON THE KODIAKS learned what had really happened. When Alex got home, he saw that the team chat had blown up. Wuerf heard Gill call Alex that awful name. They understood where Alex's outburst came from and nobody blamed him.

Alex's penalty negated the Kodiaks' power play, and the Twins had started the third period with a man advantage. They made the Kodiaks pay, banging home the puck during a scramble to tie the game. It was all downhill from there. The final score was 6–2. It felt like the season was over—but it wasn't. That's not how it worked. The Kodiaks were now on the B-side, but if they managed to win out, they could still make it to the final.

"Not with me, though," Alex whispered through his tears.

Alex had decided, between leaving the arena and collapsing onto his bed, that he wasn't going to play another shift this season. In fact, he might not play hockey ever again unless his family moved back to Norway House. None of what had happened this season would have ever happened playing for the North Stars.

Alex typed two words into the team chat.

I QUIT.

He threw his tablet on the foot of his bed, curled up into a ball in the darkness, and started to cry all over again.

He cried himself to sleep.

Alex slept in late the next morning. He slept in so late that it was a stretch to call it morning when he woke up. In fact, when he opened his eyes, it was lunchtime. His stomach growled angrily, but he was too sad to eat. He thought he might just stay in bed all day, until school tomorrow. He lay there for another hour, hardly moving, in his dark room with the curtains drawn. But then, there was a knock on Alex's door. He figured it was his mom or dad bringing him food, knowing that he hadn't eaten since before last night's game.

"Go away," Alex said weakly. There were feet on the other side of the door and they weren't moving. He rolled his damp, swollen eyes, sore from crying so much last night, and said, "Just leave it outside my door then."

There was another knock.

"It's good to know you're alive in there," Mom said. "Somebody is here to see you."

The bedroom door opened. Standing in the doorway was a silhouette instantly recognizable as Wuerf. He flicked on the light, entered the room, and sat beside Alex, patting his shoulder to comfort him. That made Alex feel so guilty. Aidan was trying to make him feel better, when Alex might have cost his team the season.

"Thanks," Alex said. "I'm fine. I just feel like an idiot."

"Don't," Wuerf said. "I would've pushed him, too. I wanted to when I heard what he said."

"It totally screwed up the game for us," Alex looked down and mumbled. "We were going to win."

"Probably, but we didn't, so what are you going to do?" Wuerf said.

Alex looked at Aidan's face for the first time, just quickly, and then away.

"I told everybody what I was going to do already," Alex said. "I'm going to tell Coach that I quit. Everybody was being so mean and I don't..." He stopped himself from crying. "I'm not going somewhere I know people are going to say those things to me."

"You can't quit, Robby," Aidan said.

"Why not?" Alex asked.

"Because we totally need you," Aidan said.

At first, that sounded selfish to Alex, like Wuerf only wanted him to play because the Kodiaks couldn't win otherwise. But Aidan's tone said something different. It said that the team needed him because they were a team, and without him they weren't the same team.

"I just don't think it's worth it," Alex said.

"You can't let what somebody else said make you do something you don't want to do," Wuerf said.

"Who says I don't want to quit the team?" Alex asked.

Wuerf sighed. "Okay, it's time to bring in backup."

"What backup?" Alex said.

Jenny walked into the room, followed by Terrence. This was an intervention. Alex was equal parts mad and heart-warmed. Mad because he'd made up his mind and now he felt as if he was being forced to change it. But it was nice to have friends that cared enough about him to stage an intervention in the first place. Friends who, on a Sunday, would drop everything and come to his house to see him.

Jenny waved and sat down on Alex's chair. Terrence took the floor and made himself comfortable. He sifted through some comics, checked out a few action figures that were lying around, and finally, grabbed Alex's stick.

"It would suck if this stick didn't score any more goals," Terrence said.

"I'll just give it back to George," Alex said. Normally you didn't give gifts back, but the Warrior had to be used by somebody. It was too good to just sit there. It might as well go back to its original owner. "I didn't use it right anyway. I tried to score a goal when I should've passed it to you."

"That was one play," Terry said. "And you know what I meant, Robby."

"Stop feeling sorry for yourself," Jenny said. "Yeah, you shouldn't have pushed that kid, but you did. He wouldn't have gotten pushed if he hadn't said that stuff to you, and those parents were being racist the whole game, too. Give yourself a break! Go play hockey today!"

"What do you care if I play hockey or not?" Alex asked.

"If you don't want to play hockey, you don't have to play hockey," Jenny said matter-of-factly. "I just don't want you to be sad." She planted her feet and pushed to the side, spinning the chair around in one complete circle. When she'd come back around, she said, "But if you want to play hockey and aren't because of this, that's not a good choice."

"I'm not going to go somewhere if I know it's going to make me feel this way," Alex said.

"I get made fun of everywhere I go," Wuerf said.

"What do *you* get made fun of for?" Alex asked.

"Being a ginger?" he said. "Sometimes because I'm adopted. Imagine being an adopted ginger!"

Terrence stifled a laugh, but it was okay, because Aidan did, too. Alex's friends brought a good balance to the intervention. Aidan kept things light. Terrence was quiet but when he spoke it was meaningful. Jenny was somehow tough and brutally honest but kind all at once.

"I think that if somebody says something bad to somebody else, that's their problem, not yours," Jenny said. "You have to ignore it."

"And we'll back you up," Terrence said. "You just have to tell us about it."

At the all-star competition, that's exactly what had happened. Terrence stood up for Alex. You need other people to stand up for you, because sometimes it can be hard to stand up for yourself. At times, Alex had felt alone in the city, but he knew now, more than ever before, that he was not. He had three friends in his bedroom to prove it. There was George, too. There was always George.

"So whaddya say, Robby?" Wuerf asked. He slapped

Alex's shoulder and gave him a bro hug for good measure. "Are we going to play hockey or what?"

"We can't go on a miracle run without you," Terrence said.

Jenny shrugged. "I don't play hockey, but I like watching you guys. I want you to keep playing."

Alex met eyes with each of his friends. With Aidan, with Terrence, and then with Jenny. He wanted to play hockey. He loved hockey. He didn't want what other people said to take that away from him. But if he played again, he wondered what he could do to ignore it. Could he close his ears and play? Could he keep his anger in check if he heard something? He wouldn't be able to ignore everything. He needed to decide soon. The game was in a few hours.

"I'll think about it," Alex said.

"That's not how I pictured this going, but at least you're not *totally* quitting anymore," Wuerf said. "Right?"

"Hope we see you later today, Robby," Terrence said.

"After all our training this year, you can't quit," Jenny said. "I've got a pocket full of pebbles with your name on them."

"I'm not sure that's an incentive," Alex said.

But it really was.

A short while after Alex's friends left, Coach Kip called. They had a long talk. Coach said the same things Aidan, Jenny, and Terrence had said, only like an adult. He knew more than anybody else that the Kodiaks were not the same without Alex, and none of them were the same without each other.

"That's what makes this team special, Robby," Coach said. "You don't just play *on* a team, you *are* a team."

He was careful not to pressure Alex, but reminded him that he could only control himself, not other people. Other teams would want him not to be there. Not because he was Indigenous (although he did admit that some people were downright racist), but because he was a really good player who helped make the Kodiaks a really good team.

"We worked hard to get where we are," Coach said. "The kids look up to you. You may not be the captain, but—"

"You don't have to be the captain to be a leader," Alex said.

"That's right."

After his talk with Coach, Alex was more convinced that he might play, but it was George who changed his mind entirely. He was the last person involved in the great Kodiaks intervention.

It was one of those days when the internet service in the community was good, as if fate wanted George and Alex to be able to talk. Their conversation started off casually. George had started the playoffs, too. The North Stars had toughed out a victory in the first round. The game had gone into overtime, and George scored the game-winning goal, shorthanded. The defencemen were passing to each other along the blue line, and he anticipated it. He reached out with his stick, redirected the puck towards centre ice, and took off like a bullet. It was him and the goalie and George buried it.

"It was crazy!" George said.

Alex was genuinely happy for his friend, but also imagined himself playing in the game. That's where he should have been. If his dad hadn't left his job, if they hadn't moved to the city, he would've been headed to the second round with the North Stars, not relegated to the B-side with the Kodiaks—if he decided to play. Alex told all of this to George, including what a disaster the game had been.

"Oh, *that's* why you didn't answer my call last night," George said.

"Yeah," Alex said. "I broke our streak. Sorry."

"We can start a new one," George said. "No big deal."

"Anyway, if they win out, they can still make it to the final," Alex said.

"They?" George said.

"I don't know if I want to play anymore," Alex said.

"Because of what that kid said to you," George stated.

"Well, yeah," Alex said. "Why else?"

"Look at the present I gave you," George said.

"Like . . . literally look at it?" Alex asked.

"Yes, dummy," George said. "Go get it and look at it."

Alex left the view of the camera for a moment, picked up his stick, and sat back down in full view of George. He placed the stick on his lap.

"There. Happy?"

"What does it say on the stick?" George asked.

Alex read the stick even though he knew what it said. He read it to himself over and over again. Each time he read it the word got louder and louder until it burst into his mind like a real warrior. Like an ancestor had shouted it.

"Warrior," Alex said firmly.

"What do you think that means?" George asked.

"It means it's a brand of stick," Alex said.

"I got it for a reason, and I gave it to *you* for a reason," George insisted, not saying anything to acknowledge Alex's cheekiness, though he did have a grin on his face. "A warrior fights. When things get hard, they fight harder. When things are wrong, they make them right. The people who said those things are wrong. The best thing you can do to show them is keep playing."

There was a long silence, and during that silence, neither of them moved. It was like their tablets had frozen. Like the connection wasn't that good after all.

Finally, George asked, "So are you playing hockey tonight or what?"

Alex nodded his head.

"I'm going to play. And we're going to win."

CHAPTER 28

THE KODIAKS' SECOND playoff game was Sunday evening. They were facing the Bruins. Bear versus bear. A thrilled Wuerf celebrated as though he'd scored a goal when he met a newly energized Alex in the parking lot. They walked into the rink and checked out the updated playoff bracket. The Kodiaks had been roasted in their game, but their loss was explainable. They'd been rattled by what happened with Alex, and had to play without him. Even with a lead going into the third period, winning would have been tough. The Bruins, on the other hand, had lost a close one.

Alex and Aidan assessed their chances.

"It could go either way," Wuerf said. "Teams win all the time after a hard loss."

"Or the Bruins could be so bummed about losing that they don't play good," Alex said. "It just happened yesterday."

The boys walked into the locker room and the entire room burst into cheers. It was enough to make Alex blush. He hid his face in his jacket while his teammates got louder and louder. He'd never quit a team one night and then come back the next day, so he didn't know if applause was a normal thing, but he gladly accepted it. After things died down, Wuerf and Alex took their places.

At the end of the first period, the game was 0-0, and the chances were tied as well. It had been a back-and-forth game, and Alex liked that. It's what playoff hockey was all about. Sometime in the first period, as he jumped over the boards and onto the ice, Alex took a second to feel happy he'd decided to play. He couldn't imagine being at home in bed wondering about the game instead of playing in it.

And there were no more taunts thrown in his direction, from the stands or on the ice. It allowed Alex to just play and embrace the electricity of the atmosphere. The loud and consistent noise pumped up both teams. Clapping and gasping and shouting and kids running back and forth in front of the fans and signs on the glass and coffees in hands and popcorn on the floor and toques and jackets and everything else. It was magic. There was no other word for it.

The second period saw breathless action on both ends of the ice. When one team got a breakaway, the other team seemed to get one immediately afterwards. When one goalie stopped that breakaway, the other goalie stopped the next one. And late in the period, one minute after Alex sniped the puck over the goalie's right shoulder and sent the crowd and his teammates into a frenzy, the

Bruins tied it up on a one-timer off a perfect saucer pass over Joel's stick.

The roof was about to blow off the arena.

The Kodiaks took control in the third period. Wuerf and Alex turned it up a notch and everybody on the team followed their lead. They peppered the Bruins' goalie with puck after puck, but nothing got by him. The Bruins hung on for ten minutes before finally giving up a goal. Joel wristed a harmless shot from the point, but it was tipped in front by Cruiser and scuttled between the goalie's pads. Alex had loved the noise from the crowd throughout the entire game, but now the fans got so loud he wished he had earplugs. They didn't stop cheering until, with a minute left, the Bruins pulled their goalie and tied the game.

The Kodiaks' bench and their fans were stunned. They were so close to moving on to the next round and inching their way towards the final, then boom! It was a whole new game.

Aidan and Alex had been on the ice for the Bruins' goal, and after the puck crossed the line, they came off for a rest.

Sitting on the bench, gasping for air and squirting water into their mouths, Wuerf said, "That's hockey for you."

"You sound like a moshom," Alex said, "but you're not wrong."

How many times had Alex seen the same thing happen in the NHL? One team carries the play for like five minutes straight, then makes a little mistake and, just like that, the other team scores. Too many times to count, that's how many. The third period ended in a 2–2 tie. That meant the Kodiaks and the Bruins were going to overtime.

Overtime was weird. Not overtime itself, but how it worked in the playoffs for 11A1, which shouldn't have surprised Alex. There was one overtime period that lasted fifteen minutes. It was sudden death, so the first team to score won. But if nobody scored, they would play the *whole* game over again tomorrow night, after the scheduled games were over.

"What?" Alex asked, after Coach Kip explained this to the team.

"There are other games that have to be played," Coach said. "We have to end it or do it all over again. What do you want to do?"

It was silent until Alex stood up and walked to the gate. He opened it and stepped onto the ice.

"I want to win *now*," he said.

The players huddled together. Alex put one gloved hand in the centre, and everybody mirrored his action.

"Kodiaks on three!" Alex shouted. "One, two, three—"

"Kodiaks!"

The ref blew her whistle. Alex's line went out against the Bruins' top line. Alex leaned on his stick and glanced over at the winger he'd played against the entire game: DeLuca. Alex's mind flashed back to what happened last game, but this kid nodded at Alex in a show of respect. Alex nodded back.

"Good luck," Alex said over the roaring fans.

"Good luck," DeLuca said.

The stakes had crashed through the ceiling. Every time a player rushed into the offensive zone, the crowd somehow got louder. Every time a player shot the puck, the crowd gasped. Every time one of the goalies turned the puck away, the crowd let out a sigh of relief. It was like neither team, or any of the fans, wanted the game to end.

It was the best game Alex had ever played in. He'd never tried harder, and neither had any other kid on the ice. And there was no chirping or trash-talking. The respect DeLuca and Alex showed each other extended to all the players. Off the ice they were different. They were from different cultures, they had different interests, they played other sports, some were good at English and some were good at math, they'd come to the arena in cars or vans or trucks. But on the ice, they were all hockey players.

The extra period went the distance, right up until the last minute of overtime. With ten seconds left, and the faceoff in the neutral zone outside the Bruins' blue line, the Kodiaks called a time out. Coach Kip gave them two options: If they lost the faceoff, they should hang back and make sure the Bruins did not get a shot on net. If they won the faceoff, they should make the play that Coach drew up in the short time out.

"Execute and let's see what happens," he said.

Wuerf won the faceoff, so it was time to execute. He pulled the puck back to Terrence. Alex circled towards his own zone, skated behind Terrence, got the puck off a gentle backhand, and turned up the ice. Alex skated as fast as he could right at the opposing players. He stickhandled around the centreman, then DeLuca, and suddenly it was just Alex and the defenceman. He looped right and found one last burst of speed, leaving the last Bruin in the dust.

Alex checked the clock and saw there were two seconds remaining. There was no time to deke out the goalie. He had to take a shot. Alex sprinted to the slot, put the puck on his tape, then leaned into it. His stick whipped forward, and the puck came off like a rocket.

The clock ticked down. It was in the hundredths, less than a second left. The rink went so quiet you could hear a drop of water from the faucet in the lobby bathroom. The entire year played in Alex's mind from start to finish, from his first day in Winnipeg until now. All the bad times and all the good times. Everything led to this moment.

The puck hit the goalie's trapper, but he didn't get it clean. It redirected, hit the post, then tumbled towards the ice as the clock read 0:00.1. Just as the last 1 disappeared, the puck crossed the line. The ref pointed into the net repeatedly, signalling a good goal. The game was over, and the Kodiaks were moving on.

The kids lost their minds. It was as if they'd won the championship. Seconds after Alex scored, he was buried under all of his teammates. He could hardly breathe but he didn't care. He used all the wind in his lungs to scream with everybody else.

After the Kodiaks climbed off each other, they lined up at centre, where the Bruins were waiting for them. One by one, they shook hands or fist bumped or hugged or patted each other on the helmet. There was a part in the back of Alex's brain that cringed each time he met an opposing player in line. He had this nightmare that one of the players would say something to him about being Native, and it would ruin the good feelings of being involved in an amazing game. But nobody said anything bad. In fact, it was the opposite. Alex's overtime goal was epic. The Bruins' players said that as soon as Alex wound up and charged towards the Bruins' net, everybody knew he was going to score. He had a look in his eyes that nobody was going to stop him, and nobody did.

The question was whether they could do it all over again, because when the cheers died down and the players left the ice, the reality was that this was only the beginning. There were a lot of games left to play in a short amount of time if the Kodiaks were going to reach their ultimate goal: winning the championship.

Eight more wins.

Six to get to the finals, two more to take the best-of-three series.

"You can't think that far ahead," Coach Kip warned them in the dressing room after the game. "It's one game at a time."

That game was just a couple of days away.

CHAPTER 29

THE KODIAKS HANDLED the B-side of the playoffs exactly how Coach Kip asked them to. They never thought about the next game. They didn't even mention the next game until the game they were playing was over. After their epic victory against the Bruins, they played the Marauders, who'd lost in the second round on the A-side. They were no pushovers. Coach was worried about a letdown after such an intense and emotional game, but the Kodiaks got down to business after a shaky first few minutes where they gave up the opening goal. By the end of the first period, the score was 2–1 for them and they never looked back. When the final buzzer sounded, they'd won 5–3.

Game four was a grudge match to end all grudge matches. For Alex, and because the Kodiaks had grown so close, for everybody else, too. The Twins, the team that had beaten them in the first round, won two more games on the A-side, but lost to the Railcats and fell right into a game against the Kodiaks. Gill and his teammates came out onto the ice cocky, and why not? They'd gotten into Alex's head so much that he'd been kicked out of their last game. When the rematch started, they played hard and fast, but also like they'd already won. That was a big mistake. They were playing a different Kodiaks team, thanks to a different Alex, who was focused and ready for whatever the Twins threw at him.

The ref helped in the focus department. Before the game, she warned everybody, parents and players alike, to watch what they said to Alex. She'd been made aware of what had happened last game. So, the fans kept their mouths shut and the players didn't utter a racist word to Alex. Nothing like "dirty Indian" or anything like that. But Gill, the kid he'd pushed, made a war cry early in the game, which led to a final warning from the ref. Still, later on, another kid pretended his stick was a bow and shot an invisible arrow in Alex's direction. The ref didn't see it, but it was as though Alex didn't either. He kept his composure and had his best game of the year. It couldn't have come at a better time.

In response to the little things the Twins did to get under Alex's skin, the Kodiaks just went harder into the boards and battled with more intensity. With the score 4–0 for the Kodiaks in the second period, the Twins realized that everything they were doing was actually motivating Alex. He'd gotten a hat trick and an assist on a goal by Johnny. When it was all said and done, the Kodiaks had pummelled the Twins 7–0, leaving them dejected and in tears that their season was over. Normally,

Alex wouldn't have felt good that another kid was upset. He'd lost big games. He'd cried. But he made an exception this one time. When he left the arena after the game he walked through the lobby with his head up, meeting eyes with every parent from the Twins. The "dirty Indian" had ended their season.

It didn't get easier from there.

In the next game, Wuerf scored in the last five minutes on a deflection from Terrence and sealed a one-goal victory. The game after that went into overtime, and Alex scored to send the Kodiaks into the quarterfinals. In that game, TJ scored with four minutes to go in the third to put the Kodiaks ahead and they held on for a win.

The Kodiaks were only one win away from the championship series. They were playing the Railcats, a team they'd yet to beat this season, and if they somehow managed to win, the championships would start tomorrow and finish on Saturday night (if it went three games). Like Hockey Night in Canada. That's what it felt like for the semifinals, too. The lights in the arena seemed brighter. The crowd seemed louder and bigger. The popcorn smelled fresher. Alex's heart was beating faster. Everything was amped up. Alex felt like he'd had six energy drinks before the game. It wasn't only his heart that was beating hard. His hands and knees felt shaky, and his palms were damp in his mitts.

It was hard to stay focused during the warm-up, with fans cheering as if the game had already started, and the "Blue Out" looking like an ocean. *If they did the wave, it would look so cool*, Alex thought. There were signs taped up all over the corners of the glass and on the side of the rink where fans didn't sit. The speakers were pumping AC/DC.

The game turned out to be a showdown between the two best goalies in the league. The score was 0–0 late in the third period, even though both sides had a number of Grade-A chances: shots and odd-man rushes and break-aways you'd usually expect to score on. By the last period, kids started throwing pucks on net whenever and from wherever they could, hoping for a fluke goal. The only way to beat one of the netminders would be off a deflection or a rebound or in a scramble around the crease.

The clock ticked down, and the Kodiaks found themselves embroiled in another close game. Most of their playoff games had ended up the same way, except for when they played the Twins. The Kodiaks had won each of the nail-biters, and Coach Kip said that was the sign of a great team.

"It's what separates the good teams from the great teams," he said.

Alex was worried they'd end up in a tie and would have to play another full game. It was one of those contests where it didn't feel like anybody was going to score. Sometimes a game felt like it was going to be a shutout, even during the first period. Usually that feeling came for one team, though, not both. If they had to play another game, the finals would be pushed back.

The clock showed three seconds left when it was stopped by the Railcats goalie. He'd smothered the puck during a scrum in front of the crease. Coach called a time out. He wasn't interested in going to an extra period if he could help it. The Railcats had been gathering steam, and he was probably worried that if the game went to over-time, the Kodiaks' season might be over after working so hard to get to the semifinal. Three seconds wasn't a lot of time, but unless the Railcats won the draw cleanly and fired a laser at the Kodiaks' net, they'd have no time to score. So, Coach did something that caused the fans to gasp and the kids to share a confused glance.

He pulled the goalie to get them an extra attacker.

"It's simple," he said, with the top line on the ice plus another forward. "Wuerf wins the draw, pulls it back to Terry or Robby, and one of you guys takes the shot. The rest of you crash the net." He put his clipboard away and calmly ended the time out by saying, "We'll see what happens."

Wuerf and the opposing centre got low to the ice, ready to fight for the puck. Terrence was inside the blue line near the boards. Alex was at the top of the circle, ready and waiting. He expected the puck to come to him or Terrence. Aidan had won most of his faceoffs through-out the year, and even more when it mattered. The ref stood over the dot with his hands behind his back, mak-ing sure all the players were where they were supposed to be and nobody was inching into the circle. Wuerf and the other centre were tapping sticks in the middle, trying to get a better position. The ref held his hand out over the dot, puck grasped firmly within it. Time stood still for what seemed an eternity. The crowd, which had been loud all game, went silent. Alex took a last look at the scoreboard. The score was 0–0. The time left was 0:03.7. A long three seconds. That 0.7 seconds mattered.

"Robby!" Wuerf called out, like Babe Ruth calling his shot.

Aidan sounded confident. Alex leaned on his stick so that it was ready to fire. The ref dropped the puck. It bounced off the dot. Wuerf leaned into the centre. He got on both of his knees, his hands gripping his stick almost at the blade, and the puck came back to Alex fast.

There were less than two seconds left.

Wuerf, Johnny, Joel, and Huddy charged towards the net, filling the lane like rush-hour traffic and screening the goalie. Through the bodies, Alex saw daylight. As soon as the puck hit his tape, he let it rip. The puck sprang off his Warrior and whooshed towards the net. It somehow avoided all the players and hurtled towards, then into, the top corner. The crowd went ballistic and the buzzer sounded simultaneously. The Railcats tried to argue that time had expired, but the ref kept shaking his head and pointing at the net.

The game was over, and the Kodiaks were going to the finals.

CHAPTER 30

"**D**UDE, we're *both* in the finals!"

The first thing Alex did when he got home from the game was call George. He was the only person Alex wanted to talk to, after he'd seen Jenny in the lobby. She promised she would be at the game tomorrow night, but she was ready to give him a pep talk at school if he needed one.

"You're playing OCN, right?" Alex asked George.

George nodded. Opaskwayak Cree Nation was a good team. Their Junior A team, part of the MJHL, was usually good, too. That team was called the Blizzard. The 11A1 team was like a miniature version of the Blizzard, so they were called the Storm.

"I'm hoping for just some light flurries," George laughed.

"You told a Dad Joke," Alex said.

"Dad Jokes are deadly!" George said.

"Deadly as in if you tell one it's gonna seem like everybody in the room is dead," Alex said.

George went over his semifinal game against Cross Lake First Nation. Unlike the Kodiaks versus the Railcats, the North Stars versus the Fishers hadn't been much of a contest at all. Alex's old team had won by four goals. The North Stars weren't starting their first game of the final until the weekend, because of the distance between the two communities. Because the North Stars had finished first in the league, they were the home team. That meant the Storm had to drive several hours northeast to Norway House for the first two games of the finals. The North Stars would drive to OCN for game three a week later and stay for game four if it was needed.

"Ho-lay," Alex said. "I forgot how your playoffs last five million years."

"Until the next Ice Age," George agreed.

The North Stars were the favourites to win, even without Alex. He couldn't help but feel jealous about that, even though he was happy for George and his old teammates. He hoped they repeated as champs. Now that the rest of the Kodiaks' games were against the Winterhawks, it was okay to look ahead. Coach Kip would've approved. So Alex broke down the entire Winterhawks team for George, listing the strengths and weaknesses of player after player.

"Park doesn't really have a weakness," Alex said. "If anything, it would be that he's small, but he doesn't play small."

If Alex were to guess, he thought that either Park or Jackson was going to shadow him the entire game. He hoped it would be Park, even though he'd be tougher than

Jackson. Anybody on the team would have been better than Jackson. He'd said all those things to Alex at the all-star game. What did he have in store for Alex now? Or would he remember Terrence coming to Alex's defence, and just back off and play hockey?

"What's *his* weakness?" George asked about Jackson.

What *was* Jackson's weakness? He was big, tall, mean, skilled, strong, and fast. He mostly played forward but could go back on defence if needed. It was annoying that he was so good at hockey.

"I don't know," Alex said. "I guess that he's racist?"

Is that fair? Alex wondered. Maybe Jackson had learned to think that way about Indigenous people because his parents thought that way about Indigenous people. Their attitudes had been passed down like an heirloom. Or maybe he was only trash-talking Alex and didn't know how offensive he was being. It was hard to believe, but at the same time, a lot of people who say bad things think they're not *that* bad because they don't know any better. Jackson had stopped calling Alex names because Terrence threatened him. Alex wasn't sure that was the best way to make lasting change.

"We just have to play our game and it'll be fine," he said to George.

"Well, you always have the Warrior anyways," George said.

It was leaning against the wall by his bedroom door. Alex always kept it there. It reminded him of who he was and what he could do, as a Cree boy from Norway House. He would always have the Warrior, even if he grew out of it, which *would* happen one day.

"Best gift ever," Alex said.

Somehow, a carbon-fibre stick was one of the strongest connections he had to his home community.

"Even if you didn't have a Warrior, you'd still be one," George said with a sincere expression.

"Ever cheesy, George," Alex said, but he knew it was true.

CHAPTER 31

O N THE MORNING of game one, Alex tried his best to focus on school and have a normal day. His first class was math, and that was a good way to get his mind off hockey. You couldn't get less hockey than mathematics. His mind only strayed once or twice, when he started drawing nets and pucks in the margins of his math sheet. One time, when he noticed that he was beginning to draw a net, he turned it into Spider-Man. He was impressed with his own discipline.

At recess, Alex and Jenny walked to their usual spot. Alex hadn't brought a stick or ball like he normally did. They rolled up snowballs and threw them at the brick wall. Alex tossed a big one that stuck to the wall, and they began using it as a target.

"No jokes about shooting arrows," Alex said.

"That would be cool if you could actually shoot an arrow," Jenny said, "but I would never even think to joke about that."

"I know," Alex said.

Even though he hadn't actually shot an arrow before, he was a pretty good shot with a snowball. He didn't think that was a cultural thing. It was more of an athletic thing. It was why when he skated for the first time, he was good right from the start. And when he played hockey, he always knew how to play. Now he was thinking about hockey. *Thanks a lot, brain.*

"I hope I have the same kind of aim tonight," he said.

"You usually do," Jenny assured him.

Jenny had seen Alex score a lot of goals. Usually they came from the slot, where he picked corners like berries from a bush back home on the rez.

"Thanks," he said. "I mean, for saying that *and* for coming to watch us play this season."

"You're welcome," she said. "Now think fast!"

Jenny threw a snowball right at Alex's head. It splattered over his toque and he fell to the ground. Jenny laughed so hard she fell down, too.

After their last class, Alex did what he'd been working up the courage to do all day. He gave Jenny his Kodiaks toque at their lockers, before she went home to get ready for the game.

"I can't take this," she said.

"You have to take it," he said. "You're our super fan and plus it'll go with all your other blue clothing."

Jenny pulled the toque onto her head, then hugged him for a second before breaking away.

"How do I look?" she asked with a big smile.

"You look like your head will be warm tonight," he said.

"Go Kodiaks!" she said.

X

Now that school was over, Alex let himself think about the game. He lay on his bed in the dark, imagining what he had to do to help his team win. He stayed like that for half an hour, only taking breaks to respond to messages in the team chat. Everybody was pumped for tonight. Even though they'd never beaten the Winterhawks, Alex felt like they could, and all of his teammates thought they could, too. His parents made macaroni with bison meat sauce for supper.

"It's nice and lean and healthy," Mom said.

Alex ate every last elbow of macaroni, but then almost puked it up. The more he thought about the game, the more nervous he felt.

"We're so proud of you," Mom said. "You've worked hard this year."

"And not just at the rink," Dad added.

"Okay guys," Alex said. "Jeez."

Alex kind of liked it when his parents said they were proud of him, but he didn't want them to know that. He tried to look annoyed. He rolled his eyes, leaned back in his chair, and crossed his arms. He wasn't sure his parents bought it, but even so, his dad changed the subject.

"So," Dad said. "Ready for the game?"

Alex nodded through his anxiety. "Yeah. I think so."

"I feel like you guys have won already," Mom said.

"I know what you're saying," Alex said, "but I still want to actually win."

"I know you want to win," Dad said. "Your mother just meant that you've come so far. Your team, I mean."

The team *had* come far. He had come far as well. He'd come from Norway House Cree Nation, and didn't know if he'd ever move back. His dad's job had become permanent, which meant Winnipeg was going to be their home for a while. Well, a second home. Norway House would always be home. Alex knew that. He could feel that. He felt it every time he talked to George and every time he held the Warrior stick.

Alex checked the clock. It was almost time to go. His stomach fluttered thinking about the game, like he was on a roller-coaster ride at the Red River Exhibition.

"We've got a bit farther to go," Alex said.

CHAPTER 32

MONDAY NIGHT HOCKEY. Alex thought that should be a new thing. Forget Saturday night. It felt like the entire city had showed up to the game. Alex forged a path through the crowded lobby for Wuerf to follow. He nodded at a couple calls of "Hey Robby" and gave a few younger kids high fives. The little kids treated the Kodiaks like they were pros.

Their dressing room was two down from the Winterhawks. A few of their players were half-dressed in their equipment, watching the Zamboni clear the ice. The Winterhawks kids turned around when they noticed Alex and Wuerf approaching. One of them was Jackson. When he saw Alex, he threw him a sarcastic smile and leaned against the boards, trying to look cool. He nodded at Alex's hockey bag.

"Is that where you keep your bow and arrows?" he asked.

Some of the Winterhawks players laughed, while a couple of others grinned uncomfortably. They didn't like what Jackson had said, but didn't speak up. In Alex's mind, they'd all asked him the same thing. He stopped, holding the Warrior firmly in his hand, and met eyes with Jackson.

"You know, you're being a jerk," Alex said. "Why?"

Jackson looked surprised by Alex's question. Like he didn't actually know why. He scrambled to say, "Just keep walking."

"So you don't know why," Alex stated, continuing to press.

"You're pretty tough when Terrence isn't here," Wuerf added.

"Shut up, ginger," Jackson said.

"I bet nobody says anything about the way you look," Alex said.

"What's there to say?" Jackson challenged.

Alex hesitated. He looked Jackson up and down. There were a million things he could say just to be mean. But being mean for the sake of being mean would make him just like Jackson. He paused, but ultimately shook his head.

"I'll do my talking on the ice," Alex said.

The other Winterhawks let out a collective "oooooooh" while Alex and Wuerf continued to the dressing room, leaving Jackson and his teammates standing by the boards. Jackson looked like he was trying to think of a good comeback but said nothing.

Coach Kip gave an epic speech before the game. Alex could tell he'd practised it, probably after watching a bunch of underdog sports movies. He nailed it though. The Kodiaks left the dressing room ready to take on the world and carried that energy through to the start of the game. Alex was on the ice for the puck drop, along with the usual suspects. The Winterhawks started with Jackson, who lined up beside Alex, and Park on the blue line, quarterbacking the team. The ref waved at both goalies, then dropped the puck. The game was on.

The Winterhawks came out of the gates hard. They were tough to handle, maybe even tougher than they'd been during the regular season. They kept the puck in the Kodiaks' end for most of the period. Whenever Alex was on the ice, the Winterhawks' coach put Jackson and his line on as fast as he could. Jackson had been given the assignment to cover Alex, although it seemed like he was more interested in being physical with Alex than staying between Alex and the net. When Alex caught on to that, he used it to his advantage. In a battle against the boards near the end of the first period, on a rare occasion that the Kodiaks had the puck in the Winterhawks' zone, Jackson kept cross-checking Alex in the back. Alex swivelled away from the boards, catching Jackson off-balance, and broke free. He ripped a snapshot from between the circles that beat the goalie clean. After a raucous celebration in the corner, Alex skated to the bench, but not before locking eyes with Jackson and giving him a cheeky smile. Jackson slammed his stick in response.

Past the midway mark of the second period, the score was still 1-0. The Kodiaks had flipped the switch and were pressuring the Winterhawks more, but at the end of the period TJ took a slashing penalty that left them shorthanded. The Winterhawks had the most dangerous power play in the league and cashed in quickly, tying the game 1-1.

Hockey was a game of momentum. In the third period, the Winterhawks found another gear and the Kodiaks simply hung on for dear life. With five minutes left in the third, the score was 3-1 and it would've been worse if it wasn't for Braxton.

Coach Kip signalled for a time out.

"I'm proud of you guys," Coach said. "What have I said all season?" He didn't wait for a response. "Work hard. We may not be the best team, but we're going to work the hardest. If we come out of this game down one nothing in the series, we can do it with our heads high. Just close things out the best we can, all right boys? Kodiaks on three."

On the count of three, the kids shouted "Kodiaks!" and it was like the white bear on their jerseys roared.

For the rest of the period, the Kodiaks gave the Winterhawks all they could handle. Alex scored his second goal of the game with a minute left, beating Jackson on the wing by squeezing between him and the boards, then firing a low shot through the goalie's five-hole. But that's as close as the Kodiaks got. When the game ended, they were down 1-0 in the series. They had to win two games in a row if they were going to take the championship.

The dressing room was quiet after the game, but more because the players were reflecting on the loss, rather than feeling down. The Winterhawks were as tough as the Kodiaks had expected. Not many teams, however, had lost to the Winterhawks by just one measly goal.

"If tonight taught you anything, it's that those guys are not unbeatable," Coach Kip said. "They're kids who love hockey and want to win the championship, just like you. We can do this."

When the team entered the lobby, they were greeted with applause and shouts of encouragement from their parents and fans. It had been an exciting game, and they almost pulled off a win against a team that never lost.

Almost.

Alex could hear Jackson right then, asking him if he kept his bow and arrows in his hockey bag. Nope. There was nothing like that. But Alex hoped there was more than stinky hockey equipment. He hoped there was a miracle buried somewhere in there.

CHAPTER 33

J ENNY AND GEORGE both said the game had been exciting. Jenny was there, of course, and Alex's dad had streamed the game for George to watch. Parts of the game, that is.

"Your dad's not the best cameraman, and the reception sucked, but I saw a lot," George said when they chatted after Alex got home. "You guys *almost* had them!"

"I know!" Alex lamented.

In the second it took him to say those words, he replayed the entire game in his mind. Every. Single. Play. All the things that went right, and all the things that could have gone better. Every athlete did that. Alex tried to think about it so he, and the team, could improve. Improve by one agonizing goal.

"That game should've gone to overtime!" Alex said.

"I don't know," George shrugged. "They're pretty good."

They were more than pretty good. But the Kodiaks were pretty good, too. And the series wasn't over. There was at least one game left. Hopefully two.

Alex felt a flood of emotions when he woke up the next morning. He felt good about last night. The game had been close, and the Kodiaks had given it everything they had. What more could anybody ask for? His mom made a huge breakfast so Alex could get back all the calories he'd burned off. His parents finished their breakfast while Alex dove in for seconds, then watched him until it became weird.

"What?" Alex said.

Dad cleared his throat. "Do you remember when you were younger, and we gave you incentives to play well?" he asked.

"Work hard, not play well," Mom corrected.

"Right," Dad said. "Anyway, we'd give you five dollars if you worked harder than anybody else. Remember?"

"Yeah," Alex said.

He remembered that vividly. He wished they still gave him five dollars every game he worked hard. He did a quick calculation. He *always* worked hard. He figured he would've earned over one hundred dollars this season. He could've had next year's version of NHL in the bank.

"We aren't doing that anymore," Mom said.

"Oh, okay," Alex said. He'd been seeing dollar signs, but now he imagined an empty wallet. "So what're you talking about then?"

His parents exchanged a mischievous look. Alex wanted to scream at them to tell him what was going on, but did his best to remain calm. He knew they'd cooked up something to reward him for tomorrow night. If he worked hard? If he scored a goal? If they won?

"We've got a surprise for you," Dad said.

"For before the game," Mom said.

Alex's mind went into overdrive. What could they give him *before* the game that would help him win? An energy drink? No. He was too young for that. Wuerf had snuck one into the dressing room once and they'd had sips. It made Alex jumpy and shaky and he did not like it. New skates? No. He'd have to work them in. There was no way he'd be able to skate in them the day he got them. A new helmet or some other equipment? He wouldn't wear that either, for the same reason. Any piece of equipment had to be broken in. Except for... Alex's heart jumped.

"You better not have gotten me a stick," he said.

Alex wanted to run to his room and jump on his Warrior to protect it. That's what it must have been. He knew the Warrior was on its last legs. It had been well loved and well played, by both him and George. There was a chip on the heel and a tiny crack near the top of the shaft.

"No, that's not it," Dad said quickly.

Alex let out a sigh and wiped a bead of sweat from his forehead. What a relief.

"It *is* stick-related though, in a way," Mom said.

"You know how I streamed the game for George last night?" Dad asked.

"Yeah," Alex said, drawing it out in a very suspicious way. Like, "Yeeeeeeeeeeaaaaahhhh?"

"We're not streaming it for him tomorrow," Mom said.

"Oh," Alex said, his heart going from jumping to falling. "Why not?"

Had George told them something he hadn't told Alex? George had to travel for the finals, but Alex couldn't remember if the game was soon, and if it was home or away, and if it was away, when he'd have to leave. His head was too full of Kodiaks stuff. His dad didn't make him wait a second longer. He and Alex's mom started beaming.

"Because he's coming here to watch!" Dad said.

"What?" Alex jumped up and almost knocked his plate off the table. "But he has his own games! He's in the finals too!"

"He's going to come here, then go back home on Thursday. His first game isn't until Saturday," Mom explained.

"When's he coming?" Alex asked.

"He'll be here when you get home from school tomorrow," Dad said.

"He's going to ride with us to the game," Mom said.

"No way!" Alex said.

He couldn't believe that George was going to be here for the game. There'd be no crappy stream he'd have to watch. There'd be no need for Alex to give him the play-by-play afterwards. George would see the whole thing and with the best reception possible: in person! His parents were delighted, Alex was over the moon, and tomorrow couldn't come soon enough.

That night, Alex and George had a quick video call where all they did was gush at the prospect of George watching the game in real life.

"Now I totally have to come watch *your* game!" Alex said.

"My game's the same night as game three for you," George said.

"Do you really think we can make it that far?" Alex asked.

"Anything's possible," George said, which was the weakest endorsement Alex had ever heard, but at least he didn't say no outright.

"If we win and I can't make it to your next game, I'll come for the game after that," Alex promised.

"And if you score a goal tomorrow, point at me in the stands," George said.

"That's lame," Alex said. "You're not my girlfriend or anything."

"But I *did* give you the stick," George said.

"I'll do the Teemu Selanne and throw my glove up and shoot it down like we're hunting prairie chickens or something," Alex said. "That's my compromise."

"Or... you could point at your *real* girlfriend," George said melodically.

"Jenny is not my girlfriend!" Alex shouted. "That's gross."

"We're old enough that girls don't have to be gross anymore," George said. "Plus you're blushing like crazy."

"You can't even tell that," Alex said.

"I guess I'll see tomorrow in person," George said.

CHAPTER 34

WALKING HOME FROM school on the day of the big game, Alex could see a familiar van parked in front of his house from half a block away. It was dark blue with a sliding door at the back and a passenger-side front window that he knew didn't work. You had to crane your fingers over the top of it and push it down. He and George called that air conditioning, rez style. Rust encircled the bottom of the paint job. It looked like tiny flames. George used to say that it was intentional, because if you squinted your eyes it looked cool.

"Nothing's cool if you have to squint your eyes to make it cool," Alex had replied more than once.

George was at his house! Alex ran when he saw the vehicle. He probably broke a world record sprinting to the front door, but there was nobody around to witness it. Oh well. He burst inside without breaking stride, causing

George's father to spill a glass of water that splashed across the kitchen floor.

"Holy!" George's dad said.

"Alex, you need to calm down," Mom said.

"At least it wasn't coffee," George's dad said. "How are you doing, Robo?"

"Where's George?" Alex asked, ignoring the question.

Mom pointed in the direction of Alex's room. Alex sprinted off again.

"Save some energy for the game!" Dad called after him.

Alex hovered outside his bedroom door for a moment, thinking that he should act a bit more put-together for George. But he didn't have to pretend *not* to be excited to see his best friend. There was a repetitive banging inside his bedroom, and Alex opened the door to find George shooting a tennis ball off the wall with his Warrior. There was a mini-stick net against the wall, but George wasn't exactly hitting it. Alex laughed when he saw an errant shot bounce back and hit George in the leg.

"That stick works way better for me," Alex said.

"Obviously," George said. "That's why I gave it to you."

"It used to work fine for you," Alex said.

"No cap," George said.

"No cap, Cap," Alex said.

"Shut up."

George playfully shoved Alex, who exaggerated the impact and fell dramatically onto his bed. He watched as George took another shot and this one found the mesh. George celebrated as if he'd scored a game-winning goal, then dropped the stick and sat beside Alex.

"Nervous?" George asked.

"I guess," Alex said.

It was also no cap that Alex was a bundle of nerves. He loved that George was there, but his presence made Alex more nervous. He wanted to impress his old teammate even more than he wanted to impress Jenny when he saw her in the stands. On top of that, there was the prospect of facing off with Jackson. Alex was still worried that Jackson would try to throw him off his game by saying something crappy again. He hadn't said anything last game, but that didn't mean it couldn't happen tonight.

For supper, Alex's mom carbo-loaded him again, making a pile of spaghetti both he and George demolished. George ate like *he* had a game. When their mouths weren't full, they talked about how things were going in Norway House. He'd been getting nightly updates from George since his first night in Winnipeg, but Alex was happy to talk about his home community.

The conversation died off on the way to the game. It was time to focus. Not a word was said until the car entered the parking lot of Allard Arena, which had become like a third home to Alex. If he were to put them in order, he'd say that Norway House was at the top, then their little house in the West End of Winnipeg, and finally, Allard. As they pulled into a parking spot, Wuerf arrived with his mom and they all greeted each other.

Wuerf was almost as excited to see George as Alex had been. They'd met once after a game at the Indigenous Cup and had hit it off instantly. Alex had been slightly worried about jealousy—his best friend in life was meeting his best friend in Winnipeg—but there wasn't a sniff of it from either of them. In fact, Wuerf gave George a big hug.

"You came all the way down to Winnipeg for the game?" Aidan asked in disbelief, as if George had travelled from another planet.

Jenny soon joined them, and it gave Alex such a good feeling that it calmed his nerves (a bit), which had gone haywire as the car approached the arena.

"Did I mention at Christmas that you guys look like brothers?" Jenny said to George and Alex. "I mean, I don't think you all look the same," she said quickly. "You literally look like brothers."

"We might be cousins, you never know," George said. "We're all cousins up north, didn't you hear?"

"That's actually a kind of true stereotype," Alex said. "But George just feels like family."

Upon entering the arena, George and Jenny broke off, wishing Alex and Aidan good luck. The boys carried on, winding through a lobby thick with bodies, as if trying to solve a corn maze. They walked into the rink, where the crowd thinned out and the stuffiness shifted to cool, soothing air, like breathing in while sucking on a cough drop. They were in the same dressing room as the last game. Just like before, a handful of Winterhawks players were outside their dressing room, watching shredded ice magically change into a mirror as the Zamboni did laps around the boarded-in surface.

As Alex passed the Winterhawks players, he had an impulse to stop even though nobody said a word to him. He turned to face them, meeting eyes with Jackson in the middle of the group.

"Good luck tonight," Alex said.

Jackson looked back and forth between his teammates, confusedly, before settling his gaze on Alex. He did something Alex did not expect.

"Yeah, you too," Jackson said, then turned away and continued to watch the Zamboni clean the ice.

"What was that all about?" Wuerf asked, as they placed their sticks on the rack outside the dressing room.

"I want this to be about hockey." Alex shrugged. "I don't want to feel bad about the game, no matter what happens."

CHAPTER 35

FANS WERE PACKED into the stands like sardines and lined up all around the boards, slapping on the glass with encouragement well before the game began. The boards were so crowded with parents and their coffee cups and garbage mitts (which made their clapping louder) that there wasn't any room for signs.

It was a spectacle that was hard to ignore. The warm-up suffered on both sides of the ice, as Kodiaks and Winterhawks players spent as much time scanning the crowd as they did running drills. Alex got caught up in the hoopla. He started a drill late because he was trying to find George and Jenny. They were sitting together with their parents and Alex's. All of them were wearing blue, like every other Kodiak fan. Half the stands were a sea of blue, and the other was black and red, the colour of the Winterhawks' jerseys. A kid had even dressed up in a white bear suit, and quickly became the team mascot (even though it was a polar bear costume, not a Kodiak costume).

The crowd had reached a fever pitch by puck drop, and when rubber hit the ice, the cheering erupted to a jet-engine decibel that never got quieter no matter what the score was. It made it hard for the players to hear one another, but the trade-off was that it was impossible not to get pumped up by it. Alex's adrenaline was off the charts, even when he was resting on the bench between shifts.

From the start of the game, both teams put on a show for the crowd in a knock-down, drag-out contest. The action went back and forth, up and down the ice, shot after shot, chance after chance, for the better part of two periods.

With a minute left in the second period, the score was knotted up 3–3.

Alex had scored twice, despite Jackson shadowing him so close Alex found it hard to breathe. On his first goal, Alex broke loose for a split second, long enough to bang in the rebound on a point shot from Terrence. That had been on the power play. His next goal was on a delayed penalty. Alex received a pass from Wuerf at the blue line and managed to beat Jackson on the left. He cut into the middle, churning up flakes of ice so high they hit the glass. With Jackson draped all over his body, Alex managed to release a one-handed shot over the shoulder of the Winterhawks' goalie to make it 3–3.

As Alex's teammates mobbed him against the boards, Jackson skated back to the bench, dejected, shaking his head. That was the one time during the whole game that the crowd went silent in disbelief. Alex had scored what looked like an impossible goal. But it wasn't long before the thunderstorm cheering amped up again, louder than ever.

After scoring that beauty, Alex was certain it was meant to be. The Kodiaks were going to win. But in the last seconds of the middle period, Park took a pass in stride at centre and beat Joel so badly he almost fell over. As Joel tried to recover, Park went in alone and snapped a wrist shot that launched Braxton's water bottle into the air like a space shuttle.

The score was 4–3 headed into the last frame.

There were fifteen minutes left in the game. Maybe fifteen minutes left in the 11A1 season. Usually, the guys that were on for the next shift huddled together on the ice, while the players on the bench stayed in place. This time, the whole team got off the bench and gathered together to listen to Coach Kip. He didn't give the kids strategy. By now, they knew what they had to do. All he wanted was for them to play their hearts out, win or lose.

He repeated the mantra he'd used all season one more time. "Teams might score more than us, but they'll never work harder than us."

The Kodiaks put their gloves in the middle and counted down from three, then yelled out "Kodiaks!"

Alex, Wuerf, Johnny, Joel, and Terrence took their positions. Jackson lined up beside Alex and shouldered him lightly, as if to send a message that getting past him wasn't going to be easy. The ref made sure both goalies were ready, then dropped the puck.

Wuerf won the draw and pulled the puck back to Joel, who passed it over to Terrence. Alex broke into the middle and Terrence fired a saucer pass onto his tape. Alex shook Jackson loose and entered the Winterhawks' zone down the right-hand boards. Their defenceman tried to rub him out, but Alex squeezed by and saw Johnny crashing the net out of the corner of his eye. He slid the puck over to him, and Johnny one-timed it. The puck headed for the inside right post, but the goalie got there in time. With a heavy thud, the puck deflected into the corner. Ten seconds into the period and the Kodiaks had almost tied it. That trend repeated itself over and over for the next several minutes, but the Kodiaks couldn't score.

"Their goalie probably feels like we're shooting a beach ball at him," Alex said, panting on the bench after another good shift.

With three minutes left, the action was focused in the Kodiaks' zone. A couple of times, the Winterhawks nearly made it a two-goal lead, but Braxton stood tall.

Then the Kodiaks caught a break.

Terrence was rushing the puck out from behind the Kodiaks' net when the Winterhawks centre got his stick caught up under his armpit. Terrence fell to the ice, and the ref's arm shot into the air, signalling a penalty. The faceoff went all the way down into the Winterhawks' zone. Right off the draw, Wuerf was hauled down. The ref called another penalty. Out of nowhere, the Kodiaks were given new life. They had a two-man advantage for two minutes.

When the penalties were over, regulation time would be over, too.

Coach Kip put out the big guns and added another, pulling Braxton to give the Kodiaks a six-on-three power play. It was Alex, Wuerf, Johnny, Huddy, Terrence, and

Cruiser. Jackson, Park, and another defenceman countered for the Winterhawks.

Wuerf won the faceoff, and the Kodiaks began to move the puck around the perimeter of the Winterhawks' zone, waiting for the perfect shot that would send the game into overtime. But they were a little too patient looking for the right chance. Soon, there was less than a minute to go. Alex saw that time was slipping away and decided to fire everything at the net. The next time he received a pass, he tried to catch the goalie off-guard and snapped a shot from a bad angle. The goalie bobbled it, but it fell harmlessly on the ice and he covered it up.

Coach Kip called a time out. He told the kids to create traffic and get the puck on net. Two players would be in front of the crease to screen the goalie and get rebounds, and the other four players would be at the corners. They were to feed the puck back and forth and shoot whenever there was an opening.

The ref blew the whistle, summoning the players to the faceoff dot. All nine players were greeted with applause from the fans.

There were thirty seconds to go in the period.

The Kodiaks gained control of the puck. They began to pass it back and forth while Cruiser and Huddy screened the Winterhawks' goalie. Terrence and Johnny were on the blue line, and Alex and Wuerf were along the boards.

Then Alex saw it.

It ran through his mind like the play had already happened. There was a space between the circles that the Winterhawks had left open because two of them were occupied with the Kodiaks in front of the net and the other one was skating back and forth, following the puck. Coach had told them to make the zone a shooting gallery, but there just hadn't been an opening. Alex found it. He received a pass from Terrence and immediately sent it right back. Terry passed the puck to Johnny, and the Winterhawks player went for a steal, getting out of position. Alex skated to the middle of the ice, between the circles, while Johnny passed the puck to Wuerf.

"Wuerf!" Alex called.

Aidan saw Alex all alone in front of the net. Alex raised his Warrior stick into the air, ready for a one-timer. Wuerf sent a perfect pass in Alex's direction, and as the clock sped to zero, Alex swung at the puck and hit it on the sweet spot. It came off his tape and raced towards the top corner.

The cheering stopped.

The players stood still.

The clock refused to tick.

Alex could see the opening between the goalie's trapper and the crossbar. He could almost hear the goal buzzer. He imagined overtime. He imagined the Kodiaks carrying all the momentum into the extra period. He knew they'd win it. He knew they'd force a third and final game. That championship game played in his mind in the fraction of a second it took for the puck to reach the net after zipping past the goalie's trapper.

But the buzzer didn't sound.

There would be no overtime.

The only sound Alex heard was an awful clang as the puck hit the crossbar and tumbled over the net.

The game ended.

The Winterhawks threw their helmets and gloves into the air and piled on top of each other. While they cheered and celebrated, the six Kodiaks players who'd almost tied the game skated to their bench, most of them in tears. Some of them stood in front of the bench, accepting pats on their shoulders from teammates. Alex and Wuerf kneeled at the blue line, their elbows resting on their sticks, and watched the celebration in disbelief.

It felt as though the celebration went on forever, but it was only a few minutes before the Winterhawks lined up at centre to shake hands. The Kodiaks met them there. Alex was at the back of the line, as if putting it off meant that what had just happened wasn't real.

But it was.

Soon, Alex was shaking hands with the Winterhawks players, the defending champions. Eventually he and Jackson met. They stopped and looked at one another in silence, their hands at their sides. The things Jackson had said echoed in Alex's mind. Alex had wanted to beat the Winterhawks more than anything because of Jackson's words. But the Winterhawks won, and Alex prepared himself for Jackson's gloating, to have to be the bigger person. Jackson raised an ungloved hand, Alex took it, and they shook hands while sharing a tight-lipped smile.

"Good game," Jackson said to Alex.

"Good game," Alex said to Jackson.

"You're all right, Robinson," Jackson said.

"Thanks," Alex said. He paused, then added, "I know I am."

After the handshakes, the Kodiaks skated towards the stands, where all their siblings and friends and parents were sitting. Where they had sat for the entire playoffs. The Kodiaks stood in a line, arms around one another, and the fans cheered for them one last time. Alex scanned the crowd until he locked eyes with Jenny and George. They were clapping along with everybody else and didn't look disappointed. They looked proud. Alex waved at them and his parents, who'd come to watch his practices and games, rain or shine or snow.

Then, he found himself looking to the Winterhawks' side. Their parents and siblings and friends were applauding the Kodiaks as well.

There were no jeers.

Nobody was calling him names.

It wouldn't always be that way. There was going to be somebody, at some point, who would say something ignorant. Alex knew that. But he knew, now, that when it did happen, it would be their problem, not his.

Everybody was appreciative of the battle the Kodiaks had put up. They hadn't won, but only one team could. It hadn't been them, but Alex knew one more thing.

There was always next year.

DAVID A. ROBERTSON (he/him/his) is the 2021 recipient of the Writer's Union of Canada's Freedom to Read Award. He is the author of more than 30 books for young readers including *When We Were Alone,* which won a Governor General's Literary Award and was a finalist for the TD Canadian Children's Literature Award. David's most recent works include the graphic novel *Breakdown* (volume 1 of the Reckoner Rises series), the middle-grade novel *The Barren Grounds*, the children's book *On the Trapline*, and the memoir *Black Water: Family, Legacy, and Blood Memory.* He is also the writer and host of the podcast *Kíwew*, which won the 2021 RTDNA Prairie Region Award for Best Podcast.

A sought-after speaker and educator, David is a member of Norway House Cree Nation. He lives in Winnipeg.